ALSO BY MARGARET DILLOWAY

Summer of a Thousand Pies
Five Things About Ava Andrews

WHERE the SKY LIVES

MARGARET DILLOWAY

BALZER + BRAY
An Imprint of HarperCollins*Publishers*

Balzer + Bray is an imprint of HarperCollins Publishers.

Where the Sky Lives
Copyright © 2022 by Margaret Dilloway
All rights reserved. Printed in the United States of America.
No part of this book may be used or reproduced in any manner whatsoever
without written permission except in the case of brief quotations embodied
in critical articles and reviews. For information address HarperCollins
Children's Books, a division of HarperCollins Publishers, 195 Broadway,
New York, NY 10007.
www.harpercollinschildrens.com

ISBN 978-0-06-304724-2

Typography by Jessie Gang
22 23 24 25 26   PC/LSCH   10 9 8 7 6 5 4 3 2 1
❖
First Edition

To the National Park Service

THE SUMMER BEFORE

The stars are almost out. Uncle Ezra watches me set up the tripod for his telescope. I think he's worried I'll forget a step. The telescope's heavy and sits on top of the tripod, so if this part's not set up right, the telescope will fall and break. "I'm making sure everything's tightened." I push down on the top to demonstrate. One of the legs collapses. "Whoops."

"It's okay. That's why we double-check." Uncle Ezra ruffles my hair. He is the only person in the world that I let do that. My mother, Dana, is more the type to give you an approving nod instead of touching you. Which, to be honest, is also how I am.

Dana looks up from the pot of beans she's stirring over the open flame. I don't normally like beans, but I love them when we're camping. Uncle Ezra says it's eating them in the open air that makes them tasty.

It's almost sunset, and we're at our favorite secret

1

spot, on land called Hedges Ranch next to Zion National Park. We're allowed in here because my mother is an archaeologist at Zion and my uncle is an astronomer, and they're mixing our camping with research.

It's a chore to get up here with all the equipment. Dana and I only do it when Uncle Ezra's here to help carry the tents and backpacks. "My brother the pack animal," Dana calls him. We found an open field with the best view of the stars. Or Ezra did.

"So, Tuesday, are you going to be an archaeologist like me or an astronomer like your uncle Ezra?" Dana takes out a spoonful of beans, blows on them, tastes. "I recommend archaeologist so you can get some sunshine once in a while. Your uncle's basically a vampire."

"What is this, some kind of competition?" Uncle Ezra laughs, setting the telescope on top of the tripod and tightening the bolts.

"Isn't everything with us?" Dana gestures at the blanket next to her. On it sit some tiny pottery shards that we found earlier in the day, probably from a Paiute tribe that once lived near here. Actually, Ezra was the one who found them. Dana marked the spot and will take these back to the lab and look at them under a microscope. I've done it with her a dozen times. "Don't you want to keep finding earlier civilizations, Tuesday?"

"Maybe she'd rather be part of the future civilization." Ezra points upward. "Besides, since I'm the one who discovered those, maybe I ought to be doing your job, too."

"Ha. You got lucky once and you think you're an expert." Dana pretends the bowl of beans is a baseball, drawing her arm back as if she's going to pitch. "Don't make me throw these at you."

"I can find a new archaeological site whenever I like," Ezra brags. "I'll find a new one up here and you won't even know until I publish a paper."

Dana scoffs. "It's not that easy."

"Of course not. But maybe I already stumbled across one." He wiggles his brows.

Dana puts down the beans. "Wait. Did you?"

"If I did, I wouldn't give you the information so easily," Ezra says. "I'd make you work for it."

"Like one of your scavenger hunts?" I perk up. I love it when Ezra gives us clues to find things. Sometimes they're online scavenger hunts, directing us to find our birthday presents, but he's also done them in person.

"Really, Ezra, if you found something . . ." Dana looks mad.

"That's for me to know and you to find out." Ezra grins at me. I grin back.

"Ugh. Don't tease me like that." She shovels food into her mouth. "You're impossible!"

"That's what big brothers are for."

She sticks her tongue out, which is pretty gross

3

considering the mushed beans in there.

"Now, children." I put my hands on my hips. "Don't make me turn this car around." They both laugh. I sit on the blanket next to my mother and try the beans. "These are good. Thanks, Dana."

She points to the can label. "Thank the Beanie Company, not me."

I turn back to Ezra. "Why can't I be both an astronomer and an archaeologist?"

"You can be whatever you want, Tuesday." He comes over to the fire. "Don't let anyone tell you otherwise."

A strong breeze whips up, and a little stream of bright embers flies out from the fire, then goes dark. Both Dana and I shiver. "That was cold," I say. Feathery pieces of ash have gotten into my beans. "Guess that's one way to flavor them." The wind hits again, whipping smoke into my eyes, and I blink back tears. "Gosh. Just let me eat my beans in peace, wind!" I shake my fist at my imaginary enemy.

Ezra settles on my other side, so he's at a right angle to me and Dana. "I'll be a wall." And he does block the wind, protecting us so we can eat. Now it's like I'm sitting behind a big boulder, and nothing can touch me.

"Aren't you hungry?" I point at the beans.

The breeze hits again, harder now, at a slightly different angle, and Ezra repositions himself like he's our personal umbrella. "I can wait."

4

I don't know it then, but it's the last time Ezra will ever visit us. Even if I had known, I wouldn't have changed a thing about that evening.

Except maybe I would have pretended to be his wall, too, so he could have eaten his dinner in peace.

CHAPTER

1

The sky is full of secrets.

If you're lucky, you can see the moment a star bursts into flames and dies—a supernova. Or discover a new comet. Or maybe even find alien life. All because you happened to be looking in the right place at the right time.

Astronomy takes some luck. That's what Uncle Ezra always said when he took me stargazing. "Do the hard work first, so if you get a lucky opportunity, you can grab it."

Lots of amateur scientists like me have made discoveries and had things named after them. Why should I be any different? I have more chances than most people to be lucky, when it comes to the sky. Zion National Park, where Dana and I live, has one of the clearest views of the stars in the entire country. They're trying to get certified as an International Dark Sky park, but it's still listed as one of the best places in the country to stargaze. Right now I'm sitting in one of the offices in the administrative building, because this is the only place with any kind of Wi-Fi signal besides the lodge, where they don't exactly want an extra kid hanging out all the time.

I scroll through the photos my telescope camera took, looking for one of these grand moments. I scan the images with my eyes until something sparks my attention. Venus. It's not a crystal-clear image—the camera that I got from Uncle Ezra is nice, but not *that* nice.

I post the picture to my ClearNights forum account anyway. *Venus used to be a habitable planet like Earth until greenhouse gases built up and made it uninhabitable,* I write. This is a fact I learned from astronomy, one of the secrets I'm talking about. Most users on Clear-Nights are astronomers like me, so they'll already know this, but a few may not. *Do you think the Earth will end up like Venus because of climate change?* This is something I don't know the answer to.

Super cool photo, a user named CheddarBunny comments. She's a girl my age who lives in Texas and is one of my Dana-approved online friends. People on the internet aren't always who they say they are, but I know she's real because Dana set up a FaceTime through her mother. Her actual name is Natalia.

Thanks, I post.

Sometimes other planets tell us about things on Earth. Or how to study them. For example, in the forum there's a planetologist who used to study the currents on Jupiter. She used the same math to create ocean current models for the navy.

Grant, who is a law enforcement park ranger—LE, we call them—and also my best friend Carter's brand-new stepdad, takes off his broad-brimmed khaki hat as he steps inside. He's worked here a few years, but still, Grant's almost a stranger to me, and I don't like to talk much to people I don't know, so I look at the table and kind of give him a nod.

Carter and I are alike in that we don't have fathers. Or didn't, until recently, because now Carter has Grant. Carter's dad died about five years ago, before I knew him. And my mother used a donor.

My uncle Ezra wasn't a father the way people usually mean it, but he was *like* my father. On Father's Day, he's the one I sent a card to. He didn't live with us, but I never felt far away from him. He always knew everything about me—how I felt about school, which books I'd read. And he was like me in ways that Dana isn't. He said the right things to help me whenever I needed it.

He was my safe person.

Now Ezra's gone, and seeing Grant reminds me of that all over again. Grant's nice, and I'm happy for Carter, but it makes me miss my uncle even more.

Grant's freckled and tan face is clean-shaven. His red hair is springy and coiled, but right now it's sticking to his scalp with sweat. Which isn't unusual, because it's over a hundred degrees Fahrenheit outside. He takes off his sunglasses and puts on regular glasses—Grant is very nearsighted. "Hi, Tuesday," he says to me. "I'm about to go pick up Carter. Do you want to come?" He takes off his glasses again and mops at his face with a bandanna.

My other option is to go home and wait for Dana. But it's only four thirty and she doesn't get off until six. She's out "in the field" today, doing research.

He smiles at me. He gets lines around his eyes and mouth when he smiles, indenting his brown freckles and cinnamon-colored skin. I wonder if he gets wrinkle cream ads like the ones that pop up on Dana's computer. But they only ever show wrinkles on women.

"Do your wrinkle cream ads show men?" I ask him.

Now his forehead crinkles. "What?"

I realize I've skipped ahead in my mind, and of course he can't follow me. I do that sometimes. "Sorry." I remember what he actually said and try to respond to that. "Yes, I would like to go with you to pick up Carter."

"Okay." He jangles the ring of keys on his brown belt. "Delilah's right outside."

He pushes open the glass door, and I follow him into the bright, hot sunshine. Delilah is not a person, as I thought when Grant first mentioned the name. It's his red Jeep. "It's cheesy, but what can you do?" Carter said when he told me.

The Jeep has doors, but there's only a metal frame above us. I climb into the passenger side and buckle my seat belt. Grant hands me a broad-brimmed hat to put on, since the sun will burn my somewhat pale skin within twenty minutes. "You good?" He starts Delilah.

"Yes." I grab the bar above the front window where it meets the frame, because though Grant is a careful driver, being in the Jeep makes me feel like I'm on a roller coaster that's lost its brakes. And I don't even like regular roller coasters.

2

I t takes almost twenty minutes to get out of the park today, though we're traveling less than a mile. Cars keep pulling off to take photos of the canyon walls—I can't exactly blame them for that. They're pretty impressive, especially when you first see them.

A long time ago, during the Jurassic era, this was nothing but sand dunes—a desert. Those dunes are what eventually turned into the canyon walls. Millions of years of water and wind have exposed the sandstone's layers, in rusty red, pink-orange, and beach white at the top. From far away, the sandstone looks like it has lots of pockmarks and indents—when you get closer, you can see that there are some caves and cliffs in the walls.

The lowest point of the canyon is more than three thousand feet deep, and the tallest peak is more than eight thousand high, so when you're in Zion, you feel very small—especially if you go into one of the tighter spots in the canyon, like the Narrows. In the bright sun, the walls remind me of rainbow sherbet.

Once I got used to seeing the walls, though, I stopped noticing them. Dana says that's a thing that happens. Like if you hang a new poster in your room, at first you keep thinking, "Ah, what a great new picture!" but eventually you get used to seeing it and no longer notice it much.

When we go to another place for a while and come back to Zion, though, it's like seeing it all fresh again. Minds are weird like that.

The other weird thing that happens, at least to me, is when we go to another city—especially Las Vegas, which is the closest big one—I can't stand how everything smells. It's like living where the strongest scent is campfire smoke has made my nose get used to only pure air. Dana says that's not something she notices, so maybe it's only me. One of my secret useless superpowers, Uncle Ezra called it. His secret useless superpower was always picking the slowest line in the grocery store. Dana's useless superpower is picking fruit that has an unseen bruise on the inside.

There's a bunch of cars with black-tinted windows parked all together in the visitor lot and people with walkie-talkies talking to the park rangers. "Some Instagram celebrity's visiting," Grant says. "Lyla Redding."

It's not surprising that I don't know who that is. I

don't follow that kind of stuff—it's not interesting to me. Plus, ever since Dana and Uncle Ezra and I watched a documentary about how social media is designed to basically suck out your brain and sell it to companies, I haven't had any desire to use it. "There are already so many visitors. I hope she doesn't make the park even more popular." We're now stuck waiting to make a left turn onto the main road, behind a long line of tourists.

Carter's taking a rock-climbing class that's held on Hedges Ranch. Four generations ago—which would be like my great-great-grandparents' age—some man named Charles Hedges purchased four thousand acres of land next to Zion. He kept it all wilderness, and it's stayed in his family ever since. One of his great-grandsons began letting people use parts of it for a fee, so that's where Carter's doing his rock climbing.

This is also where Uncle Ezra and my mother and I used to go camping. Where Ezra took me stargazing. Where there are tons of important archaeological sites. The ranch is as important to me as Zion—maybe even more so, because so much of the ranch is what they call pristine. That means it's untouched, which is almost impossible to find anywhere, even inside a national park.

Aside from the rock-climbing area, most of Hedges is off-limits to the public. You can either do the rock-climbing class, which isn't very far inside, or you need written permission, which is what my mother has.

I'm not sure how it works for anyone else.

I don't know how it'll work in the future, either, because Hedges is actually for sale. It's been for sale for two months, ever since the owner died and his heirs decided they couldn't take care of it anymore. Or they don't *want* to take care of it anymore. I'm not sure which, or if it even matters.

We ride two minutes along the road, then turn left under a log arch that says *Hedges Ranch* in old-timey wood-burned font. The *For Sale* sign next to the arch now has a *Sold* sign above it. I turn to Grant. "It sold already?"

Grant nods. "A few weeks ago. They just made it public."

My heart does a double thump. "Who bought it? Will they keep it the same?" I hope it's someone like the Hedges family, who liked the land as it is and also allowed some use. It would be terrible if someone came here and built skyscrapers or a mall or something. Everything would be different.

Not to mention, that ranch is my special place. Where the best memories of Uncle Ezra and me and my mom all are. No place I've ever been is so still, so peaceful. Whenever I'm there, I think about how many millions of years it took for the land to look like this, all the people who once lived there, like the Paiute tribe, and it feels like I'm one small piece of a bigger puzzle. "Some people have religion," Uncle Ezra said, the last time we were there, "but this is our church."

"I'm not sure." Grant drives up the gravel road, sending a cloud of gray-white dust churning behind us. "If there's one thing you can count on in life, it's that it'll change."

Change. A thick feeling comes into my throat. First we lose Uncle Ezra. And now we're losing this land. "Change has not been good for me lately."

"Think positively." He chuckles. "Like me, going from being alone to having a full family all in one day."

Grant makes it sound like he met and married Carter's mom on one day. I furrow my brow. "Didn't you date Jenny for a year before you got married?"

"Yes, but . . ." He shakes his head. "I meant the marriage ceremony was a day."

The ceremony was actually only twenty-three minutes, but I think I get it. "Oh," I say.

He doesn't respond to this, and we drive in silence to where the rock climbers are waiting for their parents. Carter waves us down, and Grant stops. "Hey." Carter flings his gear into the back, then climbs in. His medium-pale skin is flushed red. He takes off his baseball cap and runs his fingers through his brown hair.

"Hay is for horses," Grant says, almost automatically, and Carter and I roll our eyes at each other.

"Camp was awesome today! We bouldered—no harnesses. I climbed a twenty-foot rock!" Carter brags. "But don't worry. They had crash pads for us to fall into."

"I would expect so." Grant does a U-turn. "I'm not paying for you to perish in a bouldering incident. You can do that for free."

"Ha ha," Carter says.

I shudder at the thought of being twenty feet up, no rope. Clinging to the boulders with only sticky-soled shoes and chalk-dusted fingers. I hate heights. "Better you than me."

"It's fun," he says. "There are a few kids who said they were afraid of heights but managed twelve feet. I bet you'd like it."

I adjust the big hat on my head and squint against the sun. "No thanks. I burn easily."

"Wear sunblock," Carter says.

This sounds like something Uncle Ezra would tell me. In fact, Carter is a lot like Uncle Ezra was. They both liked climbing rocks. They're both kind of fearless when it comes to doing outdoorsy stuff. And they both liked pushing me to do new things.

I guess that's one reason I like Carter.

Besides, he's the only other kid near my age living in the park. But even if there were a hundred kids here, I think we'd still be friends.

We drive on into Zion, and then Grant parks Delilah next to the ranger station. "I've got to go finish my shift. I'll be home in an hour or so, and we'll go get your mother." Jenny's an LE, too—she's working at the other end of the park today and will get off later.

"See you." The two of them fist-bump, even though they'll see each other again soon. I only fist-bump people if I'm not going to see them for a while.

Now Carter and I will walk to my house, in the residential community for workers near Watchman, the name of one of the mountains. He'll come in, and we'll make mac and cheese. Then we'll play a game or work on the thousand-piece *Star Wars* puzzle I got for my birthday.

I wipe sweat off my forehead as we come out from the underpass. The sun blazes off the red-and-gray-pink rock formations that form the walls of the valley where we live. Luckily, a variety of trees helps provide some shade. Zion has unusual ecology. We have both desert trees like mesquite and piñon, and high-altitude trees like fir.

Carter's telling me all about bouldering. "And look at the muscles I'm building!" He flexes his arm, which has a very small muscle on it. It's like a gopher hill on a plain, not a mountain.

I'm not sure why he's surprised. "That's what happens when you use those muscles a lot," I tell him. "They get bigger. It's science."

He sighs.

"Science never lets us down." Another thing Uncle

Ezra would say, and so the words feel good in my mouth. But uneasiness pulls at me—maybe that wasn't how Carter wanted me to react. Sometimes I say the wrong thing and don't know it. I try to think about how people will react first, but it doesn't always work. "What did you want me to say about your muscles?" I wonder out loud to him.

"A compliment?" Carter claps me on the back. "It doesn't matter, though."

When Carter lets something like that go, I tend to let it go, too. "Let's go make some mac and cheese," I say, and we turn up the road to the housing units.

Carter and I are pretty different, and sometimes being different means *making allowances for each other*, as Dana says. So Carter lets me be me, and I let Carter be Carter. Even though being Carter means he likes to pretend to be Spider-Man, crawling around on cave walls and up cliffs, I wouldn't ask him to stop. And he'd never tell me to stay inside at night instead of looking at stars.

We pass by the barracks, where the seasonal workers live in bunk beds, six to a room. There's a group of five botanists sitting at a picnic table, playing Magic: The Gathering. "Hi, Tuesday! Hi, Carter!" calls Megan, a twenty-year-old with short bleached blond hair, and I manage to give her the quickest nod. "Want to join?" Megan flaps the cards at us like a fan. The botanists are

always playing things like this. They invite me sometimes.

I shake my head. "I don't have my cards with me."

"We're going to eat," Carter says for both of us. "I'm so
hungry I could eat my own leg!"

"Dad joke," I say, and Megan laughs.

"Touché," Carter says.

"If you change your mind, we'll be playing until the
mosquitoes chase us inside." Megan turns back to her
cards.

I hesitate. Megan's so nice. It would be good to have
some social time. I'm supposed to try to get a little every
day, the same way I'm supposed to try to include all the
food groups in my meals. And Carter's so busy that I
really should try to get to know other people. That's
what Dana says, anyway.

"What if we play, just for a bit?" I whisper to Carter.

"That's cool. I actually had a snack at camp, but I
thought you didn't want to play," Carter says.

"Thanks." I smile at him. He knows me so well. We
both turn back.

"That was a close one," one of the men, Nick, says.

I freeze.

"Dana asked me to keep an eye out for her," Megan
says. "Besides, you just don't like her because she's
smarter than you."

"No. I just don't like her because she never lets anyone

forget it." Nick doesn't sound like he's joking.

Heat rolls up over my body. Do I not let people forget I'm intelligent? How would I do that? Pretend to not know things? That would be ridiculous.

I thought they liked me. And even worse, my mother told them to watch me, as though I'm some sort of infant? I squeeze my hands into fists.

"Hey." Carter puts his arm protectively around me. "Who cares what they think?" Then he makes a joke. "They're just a bunch of botanists."

That doesn't make much sense—what does being a bunch of botanists mean?—but I laugh anyway, maybe because it's so the opposite of logical. "Yeah. Bunch of botanists." I shake my fist in their general direction. "What's next, a gaggle of geologists?"

"An organization of . . . ornithologists?"

"A plague of paleontologists?"

"A crowd of chemists?" Carter finishes, and we both erupt into giggles. "Race you." Carter sprints off. We run the rest of the way to my house. The houses all look almost exactly the same, but mine's easy to find—just across the road from the big green dumpster—and I cut across behind Carter before he turns, and I somehow beat him, my fingertips touching the worn wooden steps seconds before his.

CHAPTER
3

C arter and I eat three boxes of mac and cheese. One for me, two for him. Luckily, Dana went to Costco in St. George a couple days ago—we only go there twice a month because it's almost an hour away—so we're stocked up. We also eat raw broccoli because we try to be a little nutritious like that.

The cottage is pretty small—a kitchen attached to this room, a nonworking fireplace that takes up a good part of a wall, two small bedrooms that barely fit one bed each, and one bathroom—but the rent is cheap, so Dana can't complain. She's an archaeologist, and her official title is cultural resource manager. She's also a park ranger—lots of people think that all park rangers are in law enforcement, but in fact many types of jobs are park rangers.

We've been here for four years. Since then, Dana has been put on furlough—that means her job was frozen—three times. The money to run the park comes from the federal government, not the state, and the park is always getting its funding changed. That meant she didn't get paid during those times. It was super stressful, and she kept talking about getting a job at a university instead, where she could have a little security. But then, somehow, before she could even submit an application for a new job, the funds got approved, so she decided to stay here.

When I'm an adult, I want a job that I can depend on. Not one that might disappear. I like things to stay the same as much as possible.

Uncle Ezra once pointed out that any job in any industry could potentially disappear, or a company might go out of business, or something. "What do you think happened to milkmen when people stopped getting milk delivered? You have to become accepting of the unknown," Ezra told my mother one afternoon over Zoom. "We can't control everything."

"Easy for you to say," Dana had said. "You have tenure. You'd have to commit some horrible crime for them to fire you." Tenure is job security they give professors like Ezra.

"When are you going to convince Dana to let you have internet?" Carter flops down. The couch squeaks and groans when we sit on it, as if it's about to completely collapse. Most of the furniture came with the house.

"Dana is extremely stubborn," I say to him. "She's against making Zion even more unnatural than it is." I agree with her. I shouldn't, because I want internet, but in theory I do. And I don't want to talk one way and act another. That is called being a hypocrite, which Dana complains about people being all the time.

"Hmm." Carter shovels some food into his mouth. Carter cares less about conservation than I do, if at all. Which is fine. I care enough for the both of us.

In front of us is a wooden coffee table with a jigsaw puzzle on it, and in front of that is the fireplace—which doesn't work anymore. But it's still there.

On the mantel there are a bunch of family pictures of me and Dana and my grandparents, who are her parents. And a photo of Uncle Ezra. People say I look like him. We have the same brown eyes and medium-white skin that is more yellowish than pinkish, and the nose of Great-Grandpa Joseph.

I don't want to think about Ezra, so I think about Megan and Nick. It's only June 2, and we have the whole summer to spend together. I don't care what they think of me, but I sure don't want to spend time with them on purpose.

I get up and look out the window. It's not dark yet—it won't be until closer to eight—but the light's beginning to soften and turn golden. Beyond the dumpster, a rocky hill rises up. Zion can make even a dumpster look like it came out of a painting.

I like watching how the light on the landscape changes throughout the day and the seasons. In the fall, it becomes sort of watery. In the summer at noon, the colors look hotter. "It's supposed to be clear tonight," I say. "Want to help me take out the big telescope?"

Carter's hunched over the jigsaw puzzle, a collage of all the Jedis. He squints at a straight-edged piece, then sets it into place. "Maybe. I'll probably go to bed early, to be honest." He yawns. "This weekend, though, I promise."

"Maybe you should take a nap right now and then we can go out later," I suggest.

Carter stretches out. "Good idea."

A car drives up and stops. Footsteps crunch on the gravel across the street. Someone's throwing trash away at the dumpster. I duck behind the curtain so I can watch without being seen, because it'd be awkward if the person looked up and saw me.

I recognize the thin man with the goatee right away. It's Silas Emerson, the artist-in-residence for June. He's a painter from Northern California, a professor at some art school. The park always puts up photos of the artists all over the place to advertise their talks and lessons. He's older than the college students but not as old as our parents. According to Megan, he's supercute, but to me he looks like any other hipster. He wears skinny, bright green pants and a shirt that has some kind of ironic saying on it. Probably. I can't actually see the front.

He's carrying something that looks like a black instrument case. A microscope?

"What's he throwing away?" Carter comes up beside me. We watch Silas open the dumpster, then toss the thing inside. He wipes his hands together as if he got some dirt on them, nods as if he's satisfied, and spins around. Then he marches back to his little blue car, gets in, and drives off.

"That's odd," I say. "He has a dumpster right next to his cabin." People come here to use the recycling bins by my house, but he didn't touch those.

"Wonder if it's something good," Carter says.

We look at each other and grin. As soon as Silas is out of sight, we open the door and scurry across the street. I unlatch the dumpster, Carter gives me a boost inside, and in a minute we're both standing knee-deep in trash.

We've done this before—I found a perfectly good wooden chair here, and Carter found an unopened pack of Magic: The Gathering cards. People often throw out good things when they move away.

However, Silas moved in only a few days ago, so it's too soon for him to throw away anything interesting.

Still, there's no harm in looking. I pick up the rectangular, rounded case. It looks like it might be a musical instrument case—but I don't know what kind. It weighs about five pounds, I think, and a metal buckle holds it closed.

A buckle? It's probably not a microscope, then. "Hold this." I put it into Carter's hands and unbuckle it.

Inside the case lid, there's a white stripe with initials written in black Sharpie—KM. A big boxy camera is nestled inside, an old-timey-looking one made of wood, the kind they had to put on tripods or something. It's pretty light, maybe two pounds. A hinge on the top back unlatches to reveal a big round glass thing. Attached to that is something that looks like an accordion that unfolds out to the front lens.

"Is that a telescope?" Carter says.

"It's a camera."

"Oh." Carter's forehead creases. "I don't think I've ever seen one like that."

"Me neither. But I'm pretty sure that's what it is." I pick it up and look at the lens, and the big glass panel in the back. "No cracks," I report, though I don't know if that would make a difference.

Carter boosts me out, hands the camera over, and then clambers out on his own like a monkey. "Let's have a look."

We examine the whole thing. It doesn't look broken, but maybe something's wrong on the inside. There are also ten thin metal frames that are the same size as the glass panel in the back. "Interesting. This must be where you put film. I don't see any other spot for it."

"Oh boy. Finders keepers," Carter says. "I wonder if we can get film for it."

But then my mother's small, sensible brown SUV rounds the corner and stops in front of us. The window rolls down.

"What do you have there?" Dana calls.

CHAPTER 4

Dana is very concerned about the camera. "Wooden cameras like these are very expensive. We should take it to Silas and ask if he meant to throw it out."

"He did. We saw him. It's not like someone stole it from him and threw it away." I don't understand what the problem is.

"That's right," Carter says. "Why the heck would anyone throw something away if they wanted to keep it?"

"Regardless. Tomorrow we'll go check with him. Then if he doesn't want it, you can keep it. Though I have no idea how to use it properly. It's a four-by-five—that's the size of the film. Four inches by five inches."

Delilah comes up the street, and Grant double-taps the horn. We say goodbye.

Dana is pretty sweaty, with pit stains on her T-shirt and mud all over her pants and boots.

She gathers up her long, dark red hair and secures

it in a ponytail. Unlike Grant's, the red in her hair is not natural, but the result of the henna dye kit she uses every six weeks. It's very shiny. Without it, her hair's a dull brown, same as mine. Her tan skin, a shade darker than mine, has no makeup—she says it gets sweated off—and she's wearing a khaki park uniform that makes her look like a UPS driver. I hope she's not too tired to play gin rummy with me after dinner.

"Ugh. The park is so crowded these days. I might as well be living in New York." She washes her hands at the kitchen sink.

"That seems like an exaggeration," I say to her.

"It is, but still. Maybe it's time to go somewhere else." She turns off the water, not noticing how her words have made me clench my hands into fists. "Or start planning it, anyway."

"Why would you want to move? You have a bunch of new projects that just got approved." My heart beats faster. "You'd have to start all over."

"Nobody's moving anywhere yet. Calm down." Dana smiles, but half-heartedly, at me. It's not very convincing. Ever since Ezra died, none of her happy expressions have been that convincing, to be honest. It's like she's a Dana puppet, going through motions of things that look normal. But I know her well enough to see through it.

Carter said after his father died, his mother was kind of the same way. She wanted to move, start fresh in a place where there were no memories of Carter's dad. That's why they moved to Zion. I stare at Dana. "I don't want to move."

"This isn't a conversation we need to have right now. I'm sorry I said anything." She grabs a bowl and fills it with granola, then splashes on some oat milk.

"Did you find any new artifacts?" I ask her. This area has a lot of Native American sites, both ancient and more modern, but right now she's working on one that was left by Mormon farmers in Hedges Ranch in the 1800s. There are also remnants of their housing over there. That's another reason why Hedges is so important. I ask another question before she can answer the first. "Did you know that Hedges sold?"

She nods. "I heard last week."

"Why didn't you say anything?" This hurts, not so much because of that information, but because it feels like it means my mother and I aren't close enough for her to share with me.

"I wasn't supposed to." She shakes her head. "It's going to be terrible, to be honest. They're going to build basically a whole new town."

A shock of cold floods my whole body. "How can they do that? It's wilderness!" I think of the flat plain where Dana, Ezra, and I camped. It's true, a house there with a view of the sky like that would be awesome. But I wouldn't want to steal all that view for myself. Ezra said we should always try to do things to benefit more people, instead of ourselves. "Uncle Ezra would be so mad." My voice gets louder. "That was our spot!"

"There's nothing you can do about it, Tuesday. Let's talk about something else. How was your day?" Dana spoons granola into her mouth. "Did you hang out with the botanists?"

This makes me forget about Hedges for a second. I think about Nick—I won't tell her what he said. She might get mad at him and tell him off, and that would kind of prove his point. That I'm a little kid who needs older people to look after her.

Worse, I wonder if Nick is right. If I do act like I'm smarter than other people. "Did you tell the botanists to babysit me?"

"Not babysit." Dana stirs her cereal. I notice she doesn't look at me, which means she's not entirely telling the truth. "I asked them to *look in* on you. You're alone a lot."

The worst part is, I thought the botanists wanted to hang out with me because I was a friend—or as much of a friend as I could be. But instead, I was an obligation. Another chore on their list.

Nobody wants to be somebody's chore. It's embarrassing.

I pick up the dish towel. This one has a picture of a jalapeño on it and it says, *Don't make me get jalapeño your business.* I had to say that out loud like three times before I got it. "I'm fine alone."

"I worry about you." Dana chews. "I wish you'd go to the summer camp."

"I hate riding the bus to middle school enough. St. George is even farther." My stomach clenches. "I'm twelve. In the old days I could be working in a coal mine or getting married."

Dana smiles wryly. "But we're not in the old days."

I swallow. I want to tell her that most of the reason I seem alone is because she's cut herself off from me. So I'm afraid to ask this next question, which I know is not how I should feel about asking my mother something. But lately her answer's always been no. She wants to work almost every minute she's awake.

Since my uncle passed away last year, she began writing a book about the Mormon settlers and Native Americans. She started digs on more archaeological sites and applied for funding so she could hire additional students. She works until bedtime; then she gets up in the morning and does it again.

It's as if otherwise she'll start thinking about Ezra.

"Do you want to play gin rummy tonight?" I ask hopefully.

"I've got to finish a proposal that's due tomorrow." I feel my face fall like that cake we made one time that failed due to the high altitude, such is my disappointment.

I rub my palm across my face. It would be silly to cry because Dana won't play gin rummy.

She reaches out and pats my arm. "One hand."

"One hand." I fish the deck out of the drawer before she changes her mind, my sadness evaporating.

Playing cards is another thing we used to do with Uncle Ezra when he visited. He was an astrophysicist, a professor at a college in Arizona, and came to see us as much as he could. But last October, he came down with pneumonia. And even though he was a very healthy individual, the strongest person I knew, he died.

"Remember the scavenger hunt Uncle Ezra did for my birthday last year?" My birthday's in April, during his spring break. He left me clues all over the place. Like a riddle I found in my room that said, *Ancient people decorated me / '80s kids desecrated me / what am I?* I knew what it was right away—there's a huge boulder that has cave paintings on it by the park exit—along with etchings from some '80s vandals.

At the boulder, he left a math problem that was the combination to a lock, which was on a trunk under my bed. Inside that was a puzzle box. Inside *that* was a note, explaining how Uncle Ezra was going to take me to the Grand Canyon for a week of exploring this summer.

"Yeah. That was cute." Her voice is so low I almost don't hear it.

I sit and shuffle the cards, fanning them together.

We're quiet, each having our thoughts about Ezra. In my head I can hear him playfully accusing us of cheating, then challenging both Dana and me to arm-wrestling matches. He always let me win. Dana had to work for it. When he was here, my serious mother became a lighter, more fun version of herself. Maybe like how she was when she was a kid, she and her brother always teasing each other.

I don't know quite what I want from her. It'd be nice for her to say something like, "It's sad that you can't go on the trip," or maybe offer to take me herself, but she says nothing.

I put the cards back into their box. "We don't have to play."

"Sit next to me while I work, then." So I sit on the couch with a book while she types up her proposal. At least, I tell myself, we're together.

CHAPTER
5

A half hour later, a noise from inside the chimney makes me look up. A squawk echoes down, and I get up and try to peer inside the chimney. Birds land on top, but I'm always worried they'll fall in, though it's probably impossible.

I straighten up, making sure not to hit my head on the mantel. Though the chimney doesn't work, at least we have a place to hang stockings at Christmas and display family photos. And a place for Uncle Ezra's urn.

The urn is a box made of plain medium-brown wood. When it got here, Dana had taken out the bag, a heavy-duty plastic tinted gray—it looked like a sack of rocks and dirt. Like something Dana had dug out of the earth during one of her archaeological discoveries. That thought comforted me somehow, as if my uncle were part of some future excavation.

"We'll put the box right here." Dana had placed it on the mantel.

The thought of Uncle Ezra being contained in a box forever didn't seem right. He was such a nature person. When Dana's parents passed away, they'd wanted their ashes to be scattered into the lake by their house, and they told her so. "Didn't he tell you where he wanted to spread his ashes?"

"No. He didn't." Dana's gaze was hard and bright.

The hospital sent along the stuff he had with him when he died. His watch with a dark-brown leather band, which Dana now wears. His wallet, with his driver's license where he's got a big fake-looking smile, because Ezra had a hard time looking natural in front of cameras—like I do.

And a poem he wrote, which Dana tucked inside the box.

It's written on the back of a prescription pad, with the doctor's side scratched out. His slightly messy, slanted writing in black ballpoint pen reminds me of him, too.

At the place beyond the meadows
On the table where we ate
In white socks we used to roam

Sitting still in darkness
Lit with the molecules of life
Beyond the owl's pinions

Where the sky lives

Is where I'm most at home

Please find it right away
To sleep there again
For a price I never wanted to pay

I take out the poem now and look at it again. *In white socks we used to roam?* Who runs around with just socks on, eating at a table? I mean, the imagery doesn't make sense, even for a poem.

Also, at first, I thought "pinion" meant "piñon"—because that's a small type of pine tree we have in the park. Then I had to look up pinions—it's *the outer parts of a bird's wing, including the flight feathers.* Why was he talking about owls' wings all of a sudden?

"I think it means nothing more than he misses this park," Dana had said. "And he was on a lot of medications. He wasn't himself."

I turn to my mother, wanting to ask about the poem. But she's put on her headphones, a sign she doesn't want me to interrupt. Did she see me take this out? Is she avoiding me? I don't know.

I put the poem back and don't say anything.

Late that night, I can't fall asleep. The air-conditioning whines in the window, and my bed feels lumpy. I look up at the glow-in-the-dark constellation that Ezra and I stuck up there after we moved in. The light's been off for so many hours, the stars have gone dark.

I always miss him worst in the middle of the night. It's a homesick kind of feeling. Like the time I tried spending the night at my friend's house when I was seven, and I woke up missing my bed so much I got a stomachache. The only thing that helped was going home. Going home felt as necessary as drinking water when you're thirsty.

But for this, I can't do anything to shake the longing.

If I were a different kind of kid and Dana were a different kind of mom, I might go wake her up and tell her everything. In the past, that's what she would have encouraged me to do. But she's hurting, too, so I'm afraid if I ask for comfort, it'll make us both feel worse.

So I deal with it the best way I know how. I grab my smaller telescope from its corner and sneak out the front door, making sure not to let it scrape across the wooden floor. I slip on my shoes and grab the headlamp with the red light, which is the best kind of light for night hiking—it doesn't bother the wildlife or blind others.

Outside, the night is heavy and deep, as if I'm under a

bunch of blankets, except I can breathe. I can't even see my hand in front of my face, it's so dark.

But when I look up, thousands and thousands of stars twinkle in the Milky Way. It makes me feel dizzy to see them, no matter which way I turn.

One of my earliest memories is looking at the stars with Ezra, though my little toddler eye had a hard time looking through the telescope. I found a comet with him, and we tried to name it the Ezra-Tuesday, but someone else sent it in to the Minor Planet Center before we could. "Someday we'll get one, Tuesday," he told me.

"What if we don't?" I asked.

"Then we'll have had fun anyway." He'd grinned at me, so wide I could see spinach from dinner in his back molars.

Every time I look at the stars, I'm amazed at how big the sky is and how tiny I am. And it reminds me of him in an aching but comforting way. Like a broken arm that finally has a cast around it.

The telescope weighs almost forty pounds, but I'm used to moving it—I don't rock climb, but I'm still strong from lifting my equipment. I set it about fifteen feet away from the front door. I have another, bigger one that's hard to move by myself. This one was Ezra's, and with it I can see into deeper space, along with an astronomy camera. I open the tripod legs, attach the telescope, make sure everything is secure, and train the lens skyward.

It's still warm, and a light breeze blows through the canyon, softly rattling the leaves of the trees. We live near Pa'rus Trail, underneath Watchman, which goes over by the visitor center and has the best view of the sky on this side of the canyon. It's wide and flat. Otherwise, the best night-sky view is on the east side, which you have to drive or take the shuttle to; and there are all kinds of cliffs you could accidentally fall off of. Or, best yet, you could go to where Uncle Ezra would take me, on the ranch.

Jupiter is bright tonight. I set up my telescope and point it that way. It's so big that I can see the bands of gases around it—they look like multicolored pastel stripes. A lot of these are storms. There's a big storm called the Great Red Spot—because it looks like a big red dot. This storm's been going on for four hundred years. Tonight the dot looks especially red—it's a rust red like the mountains here—and I think I can see the storms swirling inside. I take a photo of it with my telescope camera to upload later.

I face north. It's easy to tell directions in the canyon if you know which way the sun comes up, which is east. I look for the Summer Triangle, which is pretty easy to see. Most people don't know that you see different stars in the summer than you do in the wintertime. These stars are each in different constellations. Cygnus, Aquila, and Lyra.

You can tell the difference between stars and planets by how they twinkle. Stars seem to twinkle because the atmosphere is turbulent, and planets shine still and bright. Stationary.

And if you see a light that's moving slowly, that's most likely a satellite. These are all things that Uncle Ezra taught me.

I could never see a star without thinking of Ezra. I don't understand how Dana can. He taught her about stars, too, like she taught him about archaeology. "It's like both of us have two degrees," Dana joked. "Archaeology and astronomy." The study of the old on Earth and the old in space.

If he were here, he'd drive me over to the ranch right now. It's such a clear and dark night—the best kind for stargazing. I look toward the east. Beyond Watchman is Hedges. I can only imagine how much brighter a bunch of new buildings will make the sky. That's called light pollution. And then you have trouble seeing any stars at all. That's why they're barely visible in the city.

Dana told me there was nothing I could do. Maybe it's true. But I wish it weren't.

I splat a mosquito on my arm and flick it off. From the corner of my eye, a star shoots off across the sky, and by the time I look up, it's gone. I make a wish anyway, just in case. I wish for the impossible.

To see Ezra just one more time.

CHAPTER

6

The next morning, Carter comes over—he lives in LE housing, by the administration building—and we take the camera and walk over to the visitor center, where we'll take the shuttle to the Grotto. We go as early as we can—in the summer, the shuttle's the only way around the canyon except for park personnel, and the number of tourists can make the wait hours long.

It's only eight thirty, and the park's already crowded. The same cars as yesterday are in the parking lot again, including Grant's. Myra the park biologist is there, her light brown skin beginning to take on a darker summer tan, in the same park ranger uniform everyone wears.

There's a small woman there, too, wearing a big hat and some workout clothes that look like they would be better for yoga than hiking. Her skin is pale, with pink undertones, and she has long blond-silver hair, like she put gray dye in it. "That must be Lyla Redding," I comment.

"Oh!" Carter almost jumps up and down. "Let's get her autograph!"

I hang back. "She's only some Instagram person."

"Not just that! She's a YouTuber and also owns a makeup company. She's a business genius!"

"Why do you know so much about her?" Carter's got the kind of silly grin on his face that he gets when he's talking about climbing. "Ah-ha! You have a crush!"

"Maybe." He wiggles his eyebrows at me.

"Carter. She's way too old for you." She's got to be at least in her mid-twenties.

"I know. But that doesn't mean I can't get her autograph." He begins walking toward her.

There's already a small group of tourists waiting to meet her. "I'll be here."

Carter makes prayer hands at me. "Come onnnn, Tuesday. You'll like her."

"I doubt it." I keep my feet planted.

"She does a ton of conservation stuff. That's why she's here." Carter sounds proud of her, as if she's his personal friend. "And she works with the Audubon Society." That's the organization that deals with birds. Carter knows it was one of Uncle Ezra's favorites.

"All right." I follow Carter as he bounds toward Lyla.

Grant waves at us. "Hey, kids. They're getting ready for a photo shoot."

Up close, Lyla's makeup looks way too heavy, like she

did it to be in a play and needed people sitting three hundred rows back to see her eyes. She's got thick fake lashes that almost look weighted, from the way she blinks slowly, and her pink lipstick is as bright as highlighter. You can't actually see any of her real skin. I guess that's how people look for photos.

She reminds me of a social media person Ezra and I saw the last time Ezra took me up the Angels Landing/West Rim Trail. This trail is called Walter's Wiggles—it's cut into the solid stone in the side of the mountain and is paved for most of the way. Sometimes it feels like you're going to fall off the cliff—and you really could if you slipped. The trail is difficult and long, and sometimes the path's so steep that you can pretty much put your hand out in front of you and touch the trail as you walk.

As Ezra and I practically crawled up the twisting path, we saw a woman in a big jacket, even though it was summer, posing with her phone on a tripod. By the time we reached her, she'd packed it all up and gone down.

Ezra shook his head. "People like that perform life, Tuesday. They never live it."

"I know," I'd said. "I'm the last person you need to tell that to. I'd never do that."

Anyway, this Lyla character reminds me of that Instagram hiker. Does she even care about conservation, or is it to make her seem nicer?

In the parking lot, Carter jumps up and down like an overexcited puppy. "Hey! Lyla! Wanna meet your biggest fan?"

She glances over at us, her expression as smooth and blank as glass. Like she's not a person but a robot. She might give money to charities, but that doesn't mean she's the greatest or most interesting person on the planet.

"This is my stepson, Carter, and his friend Tuesday, the archaeologist's daughter. We all live in the park," Grant explains to Lyla.

Suddenly Carter pushes me toward her. I stumble forward a few steps.

She smiles at me, holds out her hand. "Hi there, little girl! I'm Lyla."

Little girl? I'm taller than she is. I clutch the camera. "I don't know why he said that." I manage to limply grab her fingers.

"Oh, she's shy!" Lyla gets right next to me. She smells like hairspray. Why is she talking about me like I'm not here? "Want a selfie?"

"Yes." Carter thrusts his phone into her hands and gets behind me. She takes a photo. I stand stiffly and probably look like a startled owl.

"Okay, kids, move along," one of the security people says gruffly and herds us toward Grant like we're sheep.

I blurt out a question, one she should be able to

answer if she works with the Audubon Society. "What's your favorite bird in Zion?"

Lyla blinks at me, and her smooth mask falls away, her eyes lighting up like she's a real human. "Indigo bunting. I haven't seen one yet. Did you know they fly by night and use the stars to navigate their way south?"

I did know that. Most little birds migrate at night, Uncle Ezra told me. It helps them avoid predators. But I'm frozen to the spot, surprised that Lyla had an answer. That she's a secret bird nerd.

Lyla grins at me. "Want to see something?" She turns and gets Myra's attention. "Can we see Alice?" Myra nods and disappears behind the row of people.

"Alice? Who's Alice?"

Myra reappears, carrying something covered in canvas. As she gets closer, I hear flapping from inside. "A bird?"

"An injured peregrine falcon." Myra sets the cage down and lifts a corner. I peek inside. A black eye above a sharp, curved beak stares back at me. Its brown and white feathers have a lot more detail up close, the brown seemingly lined with cream, and small dots here and there. Sharp claws grip a perch. "Alice has an injured wing."

As if to say, *No, I don't*, Alice flaps her wings. Now I see a dark red scab in her feathers, the size of a quarter.

"Isn't she beautiful?" Lyla asks. "Did you know that

the peregrine falcon is the world's fastest animal? It can go more than one hundred eighty-six miles per hour!"

"Yeah. My uncle was a bird fan, too." I smile at Lyla, and she puts her hand on my shoulder.

"What are you going to do, pose with her on your head?" Carter peeks inside. Alice scoots backward.

"No way! Look at those claws. No, only some photos near her." Lyla clucks at the bird. "You know, draw attention to the wildlife of the park and a wildlife rescue fund."

"We have to go while the light's good," the photographer tells her.

"Isn't the light always good here?" Lyla gestures at the canyon. "I've never seen it be bad." She closes her eyes, inhales. She's two hundred times more relaxed than she was when we first walked up to her. Lyla opens her eyes. "You two are so lucky to live here."

"We know," Carter says.

The photographer starts moving, so Lyla waves at me and turns away, her group of people moving with her like an anthill. Grant included.

"See you, kids." Myra picks up the cage and follows them.

"Told you Lyla was legit," Carter says.

"Maybe," I acknowledge. "But why did you push me at her? You're her fan. Not me."

"Because if I said *I* was her biggest fan, then she

would've ignored me because *everyone* says that. If I said you were, it seemed like I was looking out for you." Carter smiles at me in a satisfied way.

"Oh. So you did it for you. I see how it is." I have to admire Carter for thinking of that angle. "I expect you to buy me a soda for my trouble."

"Deal." We continue to the shuttle stop. Over by the river, Lyla's taking photos. I guess she is legit. I think about the way her face changed when I asked her a real question. Does she have to go around hiding who she is all the time? For a second, I almost feel sorry for her. But only a little. If I had that kind of money and stuff, I'd definitely be talking about birds more.

The shuttle pulls up, and I don't think about Lyla Redding for the rest of the day. I can't say the same for Carter.

The shuttle is one of those buses that has a connector and another car behind it, like a train. The Grotto picnic area is next to the artist cabin and is five stops away. I hope throwing away the camera wasn't a mistake, and that Silas lets us keep it. But I'll definitely give it back if he's changed his mind.

The bus door opens, and I'm glad to see Felipe sitting behind the wheel. He's my favorite bus driver. He's semi-retired and lives in Hurricane, about a half hour away. He comes back year after year. Most of the other drivers are hired for the summer, and Felipe trains them all. "Well, look who it is," he said. "The terrible twosome."

He always calls us this. At first I thought he meant we were terrible, and I told him we never broke park rules.

"Felipe! Hello, sir." Carter gives him a fist bump. "How's Hurricane?" Carter pronounces it like the locals do, which is *Hurr-Ah-kun.*

"Hurricane is same as ever," Felipe replies. I guess that means it's small and pretty quiet except for the highway that leads to our park. It's also where the middle school is located. Which is not my favorite place in the world. The history books the school gives us aren't as complete as what I know from Dana, and Uncle Ezra taught me more about math than any of my teachers. I used to text Ezra what he called my "highlight reel" every day—both the best and the weirdest things that happened at school.

I'm not looking forward to going back in the fall. Not without Ezra's funny comments to make school fun. Like once I told him how the Utah history book completely left out the part about white people enslaving the Paiute Indians, and he told me I should kick the history book out of my teacher's hand the next time.

I nod at Felipe. "Good to see you, sir."

"Good to see you, too, young miss." Felipe nods back with a smile.

We drive slowly up the scenic highway, tourists exclaiming things in various languages, and then at last Felipe pulls the bus up next to the Grotto and half of us file off, including me and Carter. "Thanks!" Carter says, and I nod at Felipe, because I'm happy to let Carter make the polite small talk for me.

Sometimes I think that's half the reason I like Carter. He takes care of a lot of the stuff that I don't necessarily like to do. Plus he's got ideas, and he's always glad to help me with mine.

The artist cabin at the Grotto is a little building made of the same kind of sandstone as the mountains, cut into great big bricks and pieced together. At first I thought it was a bathroom building, but it turns out it's an artist residence. There are signs all over it that say *Private*. A dusty tan dirt driveway with a little blue hatchback and a *Do Not Enter* sign leads up to it. The blinds are all closed. It's the oldest building in Zion, built in the 1920s, and used to be the visitor center and then a museum. I only know that because the Grotto is a stop on the Junior Ranger badge route.

I knock.

The blinds on the front door part, and one blue eye looks out at us. Then the door creaks open. "Girl Scout cookies?" Silas asks in a hopeful tone.

"Sorry, no," Carter says.

"It's not the right season," I inform him.

"Oh, man." Silas opens the door all the way. He's wearing a different pair of unusually colored pants, this time a rusty red orange that matches the sandstone. With it he's wearing a tan shirt.

I point at him, then at the mountain behind him, which has an especially thick white-tan layer at the top. If you walk up the Angels Landing Trail but turn left at the fork instead of right, you see all white stone up there. "You look like the West Ridge."

Silas glances toward where I'm pointing and barks out a laugh. "I guess I do." He looks tired, and his eyelids are a little puffy. My eyes get like that when I've been crying. Maybe he has been, too, but it seems like it would be rude to ask.

He leans on the doorjamb. "I'm not having an open house right now."

"We're not here for art," Carter holds up the camera. "Actually, I guess we sort of are."

"We saw you get rid of this in the trash," I inform him.

"Why did you throw it away?" Carter says.

"And why there instead of the dumpster by your house?" I point at the dumpster in question, on the other side of the driveway.

He holds up his hand. "Whoa, whoa, small people. Too many questions."

"That's literally two," I say.

Silas grins. "That's two too many." He crosses his arms. "First, what are you doing, diving in dumpsters? Second, why do you care if I throw away a camera? Third, why are you spying on me?"

"That's one more question than we asked," I inform him. "Shouldn't it be totally equal?"

"Well, I'm an adult." He says *AAH-dult*. "I get special dispensation."

I cross my arms, imitating him. "I notice you've avoided our questions."

He points at me. "Hey, she's astute!" Then he guffaws, a funny sound that comes up from his belly and explodes out of his mouth.

I smile back. Silas reminds me, in a strange way, of Ezra. Not in looks. My uncle was much better looking. But Uncle Ezra would kid around with me like that, and he was also kind of what Dana calls eccentric. Dana says that art and science are two sides of one coin, and meeting Silas, I can finally see how that might be true.

Carter shakes his head. "We wanted to make sure you really meant to get rid of it. It looks expensive, so it seemed like it might be an accident."

"I drove my car over there, got out of my car, took the camera out, and threw the camera away. Why would you think that was an accident?" He looks down at us, heavy-lidded and exhausted. "And it was expensive, but it's worthless to me now."

"Have you been crying?" I blurt out.

Silas's eyes open wide, startled. An array of emotions flit over his face, and I can't identify all of them. Disbelief, sadness, something I can't identify. "Yeah," he says with surprise. "How'd you know?"

I've seen eyes like that enough since Uncle Ezra died to know what's up. On both me and on Dana. I point in the general direction of his gaze. "You're puffy."

"Gee, thanks." He pokes at his arm. "I am retaining a goodly amount of water."

"Tuesday has mad observation skills." Carter looks solemn. "Well, if you want to talk about anything, we're here for you." Which sounds like something Grant might say and is a nice thing to tell people. Especially because Carter actually means it, which a lot of people don't.

Silas doesn't answer but turns his head to the side and fake-coughs several times. I can't blame him. If I were a grown-up, I wouldn't want to tell two kids who randomly showed up at my door why I was crying, either. "The camera works," he says after that. "But I don't want it. So you can have it. I'll even show you how to use it. Why I threw it away, however, is not any of your beeswax."

Carter and I glance at each other. We both want to know how the camera works. It's as old-fashioned as the phrase *none of your beeswax.*

"Yes, please show us," Carter says, interrupting my

train of thought. "It'll take less time than researching it."

"Come on in." Silas gestures.

"Are we allowed to?" I ask Carter. "He's a stranger."

"I mean, he had to apply and was selected by a committee, so he's supposed to be a kind of famous artist," Carter says.

"Ha! Famous is relative," Silas says. "I'm famous in my mom's retirement community. The rest of the world, not so much. But it's true that I'm not a criminal and I'm not going to harm you."

"My dad's an LE," Carter says. "So you'd better not."

"Even if he weren't, I wouldn't harm a hair on your heads. I know. Wait a second." Silas disappears for a moment, then returns with a plastic sandwich sign. It says *Open House: Artist-in-Residence*. "I'll have my open house right now, so you're officially allowed in."

"That works," Carter says, and Silas steps aside.

7

The cabin's much bigger than it looks from outside. Sunlight streams in through the blinds on the side and back windows. The first room is a large rectangle, with exposed, rough sandstone walls. There's a big drafting table with a bunch of lamps around it. Some photo albums and a photo box sit on the coffee table.

He's got two large easels with oil paintings of Zion on them—I recognize the Court of the Patriarchs and the Virgin River—except in Silas's style the colors are bright and unrealistic, the whites swapped for hot pinks, the red stone for electric blue. "These are weird," I say. "Because I know what they are even though the colors are totally different."

"I'm going to take *weird* as a compliment." Silas moves a stack of papers off the small couch.

"Wow. I've tried to peek in here a bunch of times, but I didn't know it was so cozy," Carter says.

Silas raises an eyebrow. "Ah-ha! I knew you were spying on me."

"I wasn't," I say.

"I'm kidding." Silas opens one of the plastic bins sitting along the wall. "Here's some film for the camera." It comes in a white cardboard box that looks like it might have a gift in it or something. "Now, this set up is pretty technical, and you have to be meticulous and remember all the steps when you use it."

I perk up. "I like things with a lot of steps."

"I figured." He opens the camera. "This accordion thing is the bellows. It slides out on these rails as you unlatch it. And you can move it up and down to frame your photo."

Then he shows us all the controls. "This is the shutter speed dial—how fast it takes a photo. If there's a lot of light, it doesn't have to stay open for long, so it can be fast. If there's not a lot of light, then it can be slow."

He explains all the numbers on the camera. I catch on instantly. This is the kind of technical thing I like.

"Maybe you'd better write all that down," Carter says.

"Sure." He reaches for one of the notebooks on his coffee table and a pen from one of the many rolling around, then writes out all twenty-five steps.

"Take a moment to reflect on what you've done," Carter reads. "Why does it say that?"

"Because people often skip steps. So they need to be

reminded to double-check their work up to that point."
Silas produces something that looks like a black jacket
that someone sewed closed at the neck. He sticks his
head into it. "This is a changing cape. For the film. It
makes for a portable darkroom," he says from inside,
then reemerges. He takes one of the frames that came
with the camera. "You put your film in here, then slide
the frame into the camera. Each piece of film gives you
two photos. But do you know what happens if film gets
exposed to light?"

We shake our heads.

Silas leans forward. "Ruined! So after you take two
photos, you have to put the film in the frames in the
dark."

"Can you do it ahead of time?" I ask.

"Yep. You have ten frames there. But after you're
done with a photo, you have to make sure you take it out
of the frame in the dark and put it into a box." He tosses
the jacket to me. "Might as well keep that."

"Thanks," I say. I like having all this equipment.
Carter, though, already looks a little bored. He sits on
the couch and starts looking through a box of art photos
that's on the coffee table—photos of Silas's other work.

Next Silas shows me how to load the film by using
an already-ruined piece and how to slide black plates in
and out so the film rests against the glass plate of the
camera.

"But"—Silas points his finger in the air—"if you're a careful photographer, you also write down the order you took the photos in." He produces a roll of masking tape. "Tape this on the frame and write down what you took. That way you won't get confused later when you have twenty photos. You can also take a little notebook with you and write it down."

I nod. "I can do that."

He shows me the focus knobs and attaches a cape to the camera—a black piece of cloth that goes over my head—so I can see what I'm photographing. when I look at the glass, or I won't be able to see what I'm photographing. I do this, and I see an upside-down Carter. Then Silas tells me to make sure the lens is closed when I take a photo or it'll be like I exposed it to the sun. "So many opportunities to ruin a photo. Like there are so many opportunities to ruin love." He shakes his head.

"That seems . . . unrelated to photography. What do you mean?" I ask.

He smiles sadly. "Nothing."

"Then why did you say it?" I wish people wouldn't talk unless they meant to say what they were going to say.

"I don't know. I shouldn't have. Forget about it." Silas screws a rubbery bulb that's attached to a wire onto the camera. "You squeeze this to take the photo."

I decide to let pass whatever Silas was getting at. I

need to focus on the camera. "It's so old-timey." I love it because I've never seen anything like it.

And this whole thing reminds me of Ezra showing me how to use his old telescope. It seems like it's filling some place inside me that I didn't even know was empty. The same kind of feeling I get when it's snowing outside and Dana and I are inside having hot chocolate. Snug, I guess.

I didn't realize how much I was missing that cozy, homey feeling. It's been gone since Ezra died. Silas does the rest of the camera demo, which goes along with his instructions, and then we disassemble it all and put it into a hard-bottomed duffel bag. "You can keep that," Silas says.

An older couple appears at the open door. "Knock, knock!" the woman says. "Can we come in?"

"Enter!" Silas says, and then he starts telling them about his work.

"What I try to do is capture how I felt when I was there," Silas is telling the couple, who ooh and aah over his work. "So the colors are more about emotions than about representing how things look in real life." He picks up a photo album from the coffee table and flips through. They're photographs of his landscape paintings. Many of the mountains and forests he's painted have big ugly roads running through them, or telephone wires, or sometimes even trash.

"Why did you include the man-made things?" the woman asks, as if she's reading my mind. "They'd be so much prettier without."

"Because all these things are part of the landscape now." Silas points at a painting of a black asphalt road alongside an ocean. "This is Big Sur in California, for example. The highway goes all the way through it, along the cliffs."

I study it. I guess this is true, that everything man-made becomes part of the landscape. But when people paint Zion, they usually don't include, say, the visitor center or museum or roads built inside the canyon. They only paint the pretty, natural stuff. If you'd only seen the art based on Zion and hadn't been to the park itself, you wouldn't know there even were any buildings here.

It makes me wonder how much Hedges will change with the new owner, whoever they are. What new buildings and roads will scar the landscape. How different will it all look by the time I'm eighteen and I leave here for college?

Silas's paintings do make me feel an emotion. Sadness.

Carter's looking through the box of photos. "This one is a totally different style." It's a black-and-white photo of a rocky beach, and there are signed initials in the bottom right-hand corner. *KM.*

"Who's KM?" I ask. "Those are the initials on the camera."

"Nobody." Silas takes the photo out of Carter's hand. "I don't know how that got in there." He packs up the camera, putting all the supplies back into the duffel bag, and hands everything to me. "Here. Take this with you."

"Why don't you do photography anymore?" the lady asks. "I saw on your website that you used to."

Silas smiles in a tight kind of way. "I just don't." He puts the box of photos on the table. "It's time for me to get back to work. Thanks for coming, everyone." He ushers us out, then looks down at me and Carter. "If you have any questions, you can come by. But the best way to learn is to start taking photos."

He shuts the door before anyone can say another word.

Carter and I blink at each other in the sudden brightness. Silas got upset, and I don't understand why.

"I wonder who KM is," the lady says to her husband. "That touched a nerve."

"I didn't like the bright colors," the husband says. "I like it when artists are more realistic. Let's go walk by the river."

They take off, discussing Silas's art, how old they think he is, and whether or not he should shave off his goatee. Though I'm not sure why that should matter to them.

"Let's go." Carter puts the camera over his shoulder. "He obviously doesn't want us around."

"Why doesn't he want to do photography anymore?" I ask Carter.

"Who knows? People get sick of stuff." We walk back to the shuttle stop.

I kick a rock out of the way. "He was very dramatic about it."

"He was," Carter agrees. "Some things are mysteries, Tuesday."

I take the bag of camera supplies away from Carter. "I'm good at mysteries." My tone is light, but inside my stomach's churning a little bit. The depressing thought of Hedges getting all cut up into roads plus Silas acting cold like that is a bit too much for me. It would be nice if everyone could act normal and things could stop from changing, only for a day.

CHAPTER
8

After lunch at home, I head over to the library inside the administrative building.

My mother doesn't work in this building but in a separate large bungalow on the other side of the parking lot, with all the scientists. Here they keep the doors locked. You either need a key or you have to get buzzed in. I press the buzzer outside. "This is Tuesday, daughter of Dana," I say. "I'm here to use the library."

"Well, daughter of Dana, Dana's not here." I recognize Herb's gruff voice. He works in the fees office, which tracks all the payments people make to the park. "But I'll come let you in."

I wait impatiently until Herb gets to the door—it takes a while. He peers down at me through smudged reading glasses. Herb's close to retirement, and sometimes he's a little grouchy. He walks back to his office, breathing hard. "How're you liking your summer?"

I shrug.

Herb sort of chuckles. "Have fun while you can, kiddo. It's all downhill from here. Ever since we got word that Hedges is being sold to a developer, things are in a tizzy."

My heart skips. "How so?"

"People are up in arms over the plans." He shrugs. "But you know what? Progress happens, whether we want it to or not. Can't build a time machine and go back to when everything was natural." Herb can be as dramatic as he is grumpy.

"Hey, Herb. Hi there, Tuesday." Julie, the park superintendent, pokes her head out of the office. Like the other park rangers, she wears a greenish top and khaki pants, and has a badge. She runs this park. "Herb, there's a staff meeting about Hedges today at five. Can I count on you?"

"Five?" Herb groans. "Why can't it be earlier?"

Hedges? My stomach goes sour. "Do you know what the buyers are going to do with the ranch, exactly?"

"Yes, we're going to talk about their plans and what we can do. Or should do. Or not do."

"In other words, we can't do anything, and the meeting will be a waste of time." Herb's bushy eyebrows scrunch together.

"Can I come?" I ask Julie. "I won't interrupt."

"You never interrupt, Tuesday," Julie says, and I smile because Julie is one of those people who says what

64

she means. Sort of like Herb but in an opposite, nicer way. "It's in the big conference room. Your mom will be there, too."

"Thanks," I say.

The library, like the camera, is old-school. They still use the cards inside books—the ones where you have to write down your name and leave the card there when you check out. There's a public library in town, but that's a couple miles away.

Hardly anyone uses this library. It's actually just an office converted into a book room, so it's not very big, but there's a pretty good selection of science books. I know there's also a photography section, though, and that's what I'm here for.

One of the library books is *Developing the Artistic Eye.* It tells you how to *create dynamic pictures that will thrill and enlighten!* That seems like a tall order, but okay. The first page talks about how you should separate what you see through the viewfinder into imaginary thirds.

Do not center objects because that will make it boring, it says. It explains how you can put the largest object off to one side. *The goal is to draw the eye around the entire photo with diagonal lines and interesting shapes. Choose one shape that will dominate.*

Then the book shows a few examples. This looks like it'll help. Uncle Ezra says it's fine to try things on your own, but you should probably do research to see if someone else already did it first, to make it easier on yourself.

I write my name carefully on the card and put it with the others.

A book about Hedges sits out on the table, and I flip through it. I bet someone got it out because of the sale. I wonder what's going to happen at the meeting? Will it be all talking? Will we make a plan? I have no idea. All I know is that Herb will probably be annoyed during the whole thing.

At home, I wish it were already five. I can't stop thinking about the meeting and what they'll say about Hedges. I gather the camera, the box of film, and a frame and take them all into the dark changing hood. I load the film the way Silas showed me—I'm pretty sure I'm doing it right—then open the book. The first exercise is to draw or photograph a still life. *Select three to seven objects that are personally important to you*, the book instructs. *This will naturally imbue meaning to your art. Odd numbers work better.*

I haven't seen the word *imbue* before, but from context I'm guessing it means that these objects will make my art mean more. Or something.

I don't see why picking things that are important to me matter so much. It seems like color and shape should matter more. So I gather some random things—three

Granny Smith apples, a box of mac and cheese, a small cereal bowl—and arrange them on the kitchen table, where the light's coming in. I set the camera up on the tripod and put the cape thing over it and then get under it and look through the camera.

I don't even have to see the finished photo to know it's boring. It looks like groceries. On a table. Yawn.

I refer back to the book. *Make the eye move around the frame by using diagonal lines.* I lean the box so it's making a diagonal line. That's better. I put the bowl on its side. Even better.

But none of these objects are important to me. I mean, I like mac and cheese, but it's not personally meaningful.

I go through the house and look for things that feel important to me. My smaller telescope, the one I haven't used since I inherited Ezra's nicer one, which I set on the kitchen table. A beagle Beanie Baby that looks like Copernicus, the dog that Dana and I had when I was little—he passed away from old age right before we moved here.

That's only two things. Why do odd numbers work better? It doesn't say why. Maybe there's no objective fact about it. It's more like a feeling, which isn't always explainable. Then I add one other thing.

Ezra's ashes.

I don't know if I'm allowed to move it. Dana never said

I couldn't, but for some reason it seems a little strange to.

Uncle Ezra got sick on a Wednesday. On Friday, he texted Dana that he was having trouble breathing and went to the hospital. They admitted him for pneumonia. By Sunday afternoon, he was gone.

When Dana got the phone call, we were at home. I was on the couch reading, and she was in the kitchen, doing dishes. I knew something was wrong with how she said, "Yes?" It's funny how much information you can get from one word, just one syllable, sometimes. So I knew something was bad before her face went gray and her mouth opened and she dropped the phone onto the floor.

Somehow, when she dropped it, all I could think about was how lucky it was that Uncle Ezra bought her that screen protector case last year for her birthday. "Nothing will break this phone now," he said. That's why Uncle Ezra still feels so close, I guess. He's everywhere. As though he's still looking out for us and making sure we're all right.

Dana never really got sad about Ezra in a normal kind of way. His college had a memorial service and I cried there, but Dana's eyes were dry. She was more mad than sad. She blamed the hospital. She blamed Ezra for not staying at home in bed as soon as he got a scratchy throat the weekend before.

Now, in the kitchen, I place the box on the table. Then I step back. Ezra's urn makes me miss him all over again. I wonder if anyone else could ever feel like that, from looking at this photo, or if it'll just be me.

I lean the telescope so it goes from left to right. I put the box in the foreground. I remember to shut the lens, and then I pull the lens cock button, which is on a spring, to get it ready to shoot.

Then I put the cape over me and see the whole scene. Upside down.

I squeeze the bulb. The button *clicks*. And that's it. There's nothing to look at, like there is with a digital camera. It's a mystery as to whether it'll come out. After all that work, it's kind of a letdown.

I take out the negative frame, switch it around, and put it back in for the second shot. Then I repeat the whole process. Finally, I tear off a little piece of tape and carefully print *Negative 1 and 2: Still Life* and stick it on there. That's the last step on my mental checklist.

I really like checklists. But I realize Silas skipped one very, very important step.

How on earth am I going to get these developed?

CHAPTER
9

Maybe half the staff shows up for the meeting at five. Herb's here, too, on a chair in the corner, his arms crossed in front of him. He looks like he's asleep, but as soon as I start staring at him, his eyelids spring open. "Resting my eyes."

Dana's talking to Nick by the window. This window, in my opinion, has some of the best views in the whole park. It spreads out and rises steeply in front of us, the West Temple and the Towers of the Virgin, the sandstone shining white at the top. It looks as though someone created it on a computer, like it can't possibly be real, but it is. "Greetings, Dana."

Dana turns with a puzzled look. "Tuesday! What are you doing here?"

"Oh, you know me." I eye Nick, getting annoyed all over with him again. "I like to go around and be smart all over the place."

Nick turns a brilliant shade of magenta. "Gonna go grab a seat." I imagine telling Carter about what I said later, how he'll laugh. If he were here, he'd say something like, "Do you need some aloe for that burn, Nick?"

Dana snorts at what I said, though she doesn't know why I said it. "That's my girl."

"Julie said I could come. That's what I'm doing here," I tell Dana, and she has me sit in a chair. She stands behind me. Everyone else sits. "Do you want to sit?" I ask, but she pats my shoulder and puts a finger to her lips.

Julie stands in front of a projector screen and welcomes everyone. "We've gathered some data on how the light pollution would affect the park. We can ask the builders to install downward-facing lights, but with a conservative estimate of five thousand new homes, a strip mall, a fire station, and a school . . ."

She shows us an illustration of the new community. "Roughly five homes per acre, minus the other land set aside. Could be more."

My heart does a double jump. I don't recognize the map anymore. There are houses abutting Zion, all along the eastern edge.

"It looks like a whole new city!" Herb says.

"Basically," Julie agrees. "Anyway, with the new development, we would definitely never qualify as a designated Dark Sky area. Too much ambient light."

71

Then Julie changes it to a slide with data about the town's carbon footprint, the increased traffic to the park, and all kinds of other things. This won't look anything like the wilderness anymore.

"Dana, do you have the report?" Julie interrupts my thoughts.

Dana speaks up. "The Native American tribes have already reviewed and approved the construction sites at Hedges." Those would be the Goshute, the Paiute, the Shoshone, and the Ute. There are lots of things I know because I'm Dana's kid. Like whenever any work gets done around here, even if it's a bathroom remodel, the tribes have to review and approve the plans in case there's something of cultural significance on the land. "But this was all done through the developer, not me, so I don't know all the details."

"Now. . ." Julie moves to the next slide. "The Hedges family said that only ten percent of this land would need to be kept pristine and undeveloped. Why ten percent? I don't know. They could've said fifty or five." She turns back to the overall view slide and uses a laser pointer to shine a red dot on a canyon. "This canyon area by the river will be preserved, as it's full of archaeological sites. But that's it, basically. That's the ten percent."

That means everything else will be developed.

"What about the bighorn sheep ranges?" Myra asks. "They're over there, too."

"They're not endangered animals," Julie says.

"So they can't build where there are endangered animals?" Herb asks.

"Correct," Julie says. "They'd have to stop construction and do a new study."

Nick taps his pencil on the table. "We would have found anything important by now—animals or archaeology sites—if it was there. The cultural resource team has walked all over that place." Nick sounds so sure of himself.

"Has the site been fully surveyed?" Julie asked Dana.

Dana shakes her head. "We've probably walked over it but haven't had the funds to formally survey every single acre." Surveying means walking over the land and looking for archaeological sites or plants or evidence of animals—depending on what your job is. Then you have to mark off what you've looked at. I've done surveying with Dana, and it's pretty boring.

Everyone begins talking. It's all very complicated. People bring up studies, data, and more. I sit back and think.

I raise my hand. "If we haven't surveyed everything, shouldn't we do that first? In case there's a new archaeological site that nobody else has found yet." The room goes quiet. I clear my throat and continue. "I mean, maybe it'll be too important to ever build over it, and then more of the land will be preserved." Maybe there's a huge find there. We don't know.

"We're already committed to other projects there. Those are what we have permits for," Dana answers. "We can't wander over the rest of the land. Not with a new owner. But if the construction crew finds something while they're digging, they'll stop and then we'll investigate."

"Sometimes they don't stop," Herb says. "Sometimes they pretend not to find it and keep on going."

"We have to trust people will follow the law," Julie says firmly.

The conversation starts back up again, but I ignore it. I've got an idea.

So they can't or won't survey. But would anyone notice *me* surveying the land? I bet nobody would care if a twelve-year-old were walking all over the place. I think about the possible consequences. They're not going to put me in jail. The owners might scold me—no big deal.

Anyway, it won't hurt to try.

But how can I do this by myself? I'm just a child. A fairly capable child, according to my mother. Still, I'm only one person.

Then I remember astronomy. Astronomy relies on citizen scientists to help out, too. This is sort of like finding a comet or a meteor in the sky. Rare. Highly improbable.

But not impossible.

10

After the meeting, I text Carter and ask him to meet me in the morning. Step one of my plan is to figure out nature photography and get Carter on board with my Big Plan to Save Hedges Through Archaeology. The title needs work, but I'll deal with that later. Also, Dana's working in the office today, so I can't get into Hedges anyway.

So the next day, Carter comes over at eight, and we gather up all the photography equipment and walk along the Pa'rus Trail. This is my favorite time of day—it's usually quiet and it feels like I have the park to myself. Just birds warbling their song and sometimes even the occasional bald eagle or condor. This part of the valley is already bright, the sun stinging my skin. It's going to be hot. "I heard about the meeting yesterday," he says as we pick our way across the sandy trail. "My parents got an email."

I wipe my forehead. The air's so dry today that my lips are already chapped. It smells different here depending on the temperature. Maybe it has to do with the sandstone walls. When it's raining or wet, there are often temporary waterfalls. Imagine the smell of a wet rock but multiplied by hundreds of thousands of square feet. Sometimes the runoff keeps going, so areas of the sandstone grow green algae in long stripes down the sides.

In the winter, the air is crisp-cold. In the summer, everything gets hot and dried out. It smells like drying sagebrush, and the salt from the fourwing saltbush plant, which looks a little bit like rosemary. Saltbush gets rid of extra salt by excreting it the way we sweat.

I stop and look at the river. "Looks clean today. Should we get a photo?" People swim in it during the summer, but sometimes there will be a bloom of toxic algae, so you always have to be alert and check the water first.

Carter shakes his head. "I think there should be . . . what's it called? . . . a thing to focus on."

"A subject," I say, remembering the book. "Good answer."

"Let's go to the bridge," he suggests.

"All right." We keep walking. A group of six deer, three adults and three fawns, grazing in the picnic area nearby look up at me. The buck—the big male in charge—goes back to eating and so do the does and fawns. They've seen me out here enough to recognize me. "Howdy," I say, and they don't move, just keep chewing away on the yellow-brown grass, dried from summer heat.

The adults all have monitoring collars around their necks. Myra says that the deer in the park are in groups and roam around in circles grazing all day. One of the does has a limp—from inbreeding, Myra says. That means they don't have enough outside mates. If you have inbreeding in any animal group, they're not as healthy. You can see it in everything from dogs to historical royal families. Carter says this is gross to think about, but sometimes science is gross.

Everything is pretty safe here for me, because I know what I'm doing and I protect myself by paying attention. A lot of tourists who come here believe that it's like Disneyland, that they can drink and swim in the river, and they can't fall off Angels Landing and the deer will pose for their pictures, but it's not like that. At all.

Once in a while, people die in national parks. They try to take a selfie from the edge of an icy cliff and slip, or they ignore the green-and-brown slime in the water and drink it, or hike into the Narrows even when there's a storm warning and rain clouds and get washed away by a flash flood.

"Respect," Uncle Ezra would say. "You have to respect nature and be aware of your surroundings."

Dana says it's too bad people aren't used to being outdoors anymore. That's one reason she lets me roam so much, within reason. Obviously I'm not allowed to go anywhere remote, but I can do the popular areas, where volunteer rangers stand along the trail with walkie-talkies and water bottles to help tourists get out of trouble.

We take the Pa'rus Trail for a half mile or so until we get to the bridge near the scenic highway entrance. We're actually on a pedestrian path below the main road bridge. It has one of the best, most famous views in the park, looking south. That's where we're heading to set up the tripod—which is also where a lot of photographers take photos. In fact, there are already about ten people with cameras. One lady sits with a little easel and paints. It's pretty typical for a summer day.

"Do you know how to use that thing?" Carter asks.

"Yes. I tried it yesterday." I don't mention the ashes. I'm afraid Carter will think I'm weird or sad and that he would tell his parents and they would say to Dana, "Did you know your daughter is obsessed with Uncle Ezra's urn?"

"We should make an Instagram for these photos," Carter says.

We stop on the bridge. I put the tripod down and pull on its legs to set it up. "Ugh. Why? You know I'm against social media." This might be a little bit of an exaggeration—it's not like I'm protesting to shut down all social networks—but I definitely don't like it.

"Yeah, but it'll be an art account." Carter whips out his phone and shows me an Instagram feed. "See, some people only have photos of their paintings and stuff. Some people take photos of, I don't know, bread. This can be all nature photos."

I guess he's right. "But how are my photos going to be any different from the thousands that are already out there?" I gesture at the people around us. "I bet every single one of these people puts their photos on Instagram."

Carter blinks as if he doesn't understand. "It doesn't matter if the subject's the same. Nobody else is Carter and Tuesday. *We're* the thing that makes these photos different." He puts the camera on the tripod and screws it in place. "My mom says there are only a few basic stories in the whole world. I mean, look at movies and books about love—they're all pretty much the same, right? And we keep watching them because each one has a different twist or whatever."

I wrinkle my nose. "You know love stories are my least favorite genre." Give me a good mystery any day. I love puzzles and lists and things like that. But I do get his point. I look at the variety of people on the bridge with their cameras. I bet every one of them has a slightly different angle on the same subject—this valley. "Well. Maybe. I have to ask Dana. And besides, we have to develop the film first, remember? It's old-fashioned." My heart sinks as I recall this important detail. "How are we going to do that? Do we want to ask Silas?"

Even though he said we could come by, I feel like we'd be pushing our luck to ask Silas anything else. He probably wants to make art, not deal with kids who want free lessons. We look at each other, me reading Carter's crinkled forehead and doubtful eyes the way I can read a map of the stars. "No," we say at the same time, and then I hold my pinkie out and Carter links it with his.

"Make a wish," Carter says, and I do, and we let go. This is something Carter's taught me to do if we say the same thing at the same time. I usually wish for something pretty grand, like world peace or the end of climate change—in case it works, I might as well go big.

Today I wish for something simple—that construction at Hedges would stop. Well, that's simpler than seeing someone who's passed away, but probably not simple enough. I should have wished that we could take a good photo.

"We can find somebody who does it. There's always someone," Carter says. "Maybe at the local college?" Which is still a couple hours away.

Two mothers with toddlers pass us, and one kid loses a ball. Carter tosses it back. "They're going to have town houses and single-family homes," a woman is saying to the mom. "And probably a Merchant Mario's. I read it on

80

Neighborhood." Neighborhood is a local website/bulletin board where people post stuff and, as far as I can tell, fight with each other.

"Oh, sorry about that!" the mom apologizes to me. Then she continues. "When are they going to start pre-sales? I'd totally live there. It's so close to this park."

I know what they're talking about. "Pardon me, but are you two talking about the new development that's going into Hedges?"

"We are!" the other woman says. "When we drove by this morning, I saw construction already starting. It's going to be so great. We live in La Verkin right now, and we have to drive an hour to get to anything." She pouts.

"You could move to Salt Lake City or St. George," I tell her. "Then you would have everything you want. There are plenty of stores there."

She gives me an odd look, the same kind Nick gives me. But my comment is perfectly reasonable. If you want the conveniences of a city, then that's where you live. I don't understand her logic. "I don't live there. I live here. And I want a Merchant Mario's."

She says she lives here. But you don't live *in* the park, I want to tell her. The park is special. I'm so tired of people coming in here like they own this place. Who cares if there's a Merchant Mario's?

It doesn't matter, because the mothers have already turned away. I don't think they'd listen even if I told them all these things. Ezra always said sometimes you have to know when arguing is an *exercise in futility*. That means useless.

"They're like everyone else," Carter says. "They only care about their own stuff."

I'm sick of people. That wanting-to-run feeling builds and builds inside me. I need to do something to get my feelings out. "Want to hike?"

Carter always wants to hike. It's not even a question. We climb up Watchman. The trail's steep in a few parts, and there are drop-offs to way down below, but mostly it's not a super-difficult trail. After it rains, there are waterfalls here and there near the Watchman trail, like there are all over the park. If it's cold it can be icy. But it's summer now, so everything is dry.

It takes about forty minutes to reach the top. The overlook part is table-flat—a mesa, which actually means "table" in Spanish. Trees and rocks seem to decorate it like candles and candies on a cake. It looks like a park, kind of, if that park had drop-offs hundreds of feet below.

We sit on a boulder and eat our snacks. In front of us, the Zion valley stretches out like a game board. Down below I can see our housing development, small houses like Monopoly pieces, RVs parked in the visitor lot lined up neatly. Carter likes to dangle his feet off the edge, but I do not. I imagine my hiking boot flinging off my foot, tumbling through the air to smash someone down below in the head.

I've been up here I don't know how many times, with Ezra and Carter and Dana. I squint at the view, Ezra's poem popping into my head. "Hey. Want to hear something weird?"

"Always."

"Uncle Ezra left a poem with his stuff." I drink water to wash down my granola bar.

He looks at me curiously. "I didn't know he wrote poetry."

I shrug. "He didn't. Not really." I recite the poem to him.

"Hmmm." Carter leans back. "It sounds like it means something."

"Right?" I sit up straight. "My mom doesn't think so."

"Well. She's kind of in denial about Ezra being gone." Carter looks at me sideways. "That's what my mom says."

Carter and Jenny would know about this, since Carter's dad died. But it hits me in a sore spot, and I defend Dana. "I don't think that's true."

He nods, says nothing.

"She has," I repeat. "I mean, she knows my uncle is dead. How is that denial?"

Carter swallows. "Sometimes I forget that my dad's gone. Like I'll want to tell him something and then remember I can't."

It's my turn to nod. I don't even know the number of times I've almost texted Ezra. My throat closes up.

"Hey." Carter bumps me with his shoulder. "What should we take a photo of?"

I'm glad he's changed the mood. "This isn't like a regular digital camera. We have to be careful not to waste film."

Carter pours the last of his Goldfish crackers into his mouth. Orange crumbs cover his chin and lap. "Yeah, it's pretty much medieval."

"How about a photo of the valley?" I set up the tripod, get under the drapes, focus the image. I get out and Carter pokes his head in.

"What if . . . what if this boulder were in the picture, too?" Carter repositions the camera.

I check it out. Instead of looking like a drone photo, now the boulder adds an *element of interest*, as my art book would say. "I like it."

"I'm an artiste!" Carter starts babbling nonsense with a French accent.

"Artists aren't always French, Carter." I get back under the drapes, take the photo, then poke my head out. "Want to hang out tomorrow? Help me with my Hedges plan?" I'm not sure what I need to prepare, except read a manual that Dana has. Carter can help me make lists, though.

He grimaces. "I've got plans with a friend from bouldering."

"Okay." I must look disappointed, because he offers something else.

"Grant's going to take me to do a little climbing in the slot canyons in a couple days. Do you want to come? Maybe take photos. Even try some bouldering." He smiles at me hopefully. "You don't have to go high."

I hesitate. If I don't go, I'm afraid it'll make Carter find other friends who do like doing that kind of thing. In my head, Ezra says, "It won't hurt to go."

"Okay," I say to him, hoping I don't sound as hesitant as I feel.

11

At home that evening, Dana heats up a frozen pizza, and we sit down to eat it with some salad. "Silas emailed me today," she says. "He says he found a photographer in town who still does old-fashioned film developing. If you want, I'll take you there the day after tomorrow."

"Thanks." I spear a tomato.

"I'm glad you have a new hobby to keep you out of trouble." Dana smiles at me.

"When was I ever in trouble?"

"Never," she admits.

We munch quietly for a while. I wish I could tell her about my plan to survey Hedges. But she's been so negative about the poem and everything, I'm sure she'll tell me no without even hearing me out. I try to remember what she taught me about making conversation. "How was your day?"

She shrugs. "A lot of headache. As usual."

"Don't you like your interns and the projects you're doing?"

She nods. "Those are fine. It's all the bureaucratic stuff I don't like." She sighs, then finally meets my eyes, as though she remembers she's supposed to be my mother. "Anything interesting happen with you?"

I tell her about hiking with Carter and taking the pictures. "Can I set up an Instagram account? For my art photos." It feels weird to call them art photos, like I'm pretending to be someone more talented than I am.

"Instagram? No, you have to be older." She shakes her head. "I thought you didn't want anything to do with social media. It turns your mind into oatmeal, plus I don't want strangers messaging you."

"You only have to be thirteen. I'm not going to talk to any strangers on it or use it for anything besides this. You can have the password. Besides, do you think I'll magically become more mature between now and when I turn thirteen next April?" This is ridiculous. It's like medications that double the dosage for a twelve-year-old. It shouldn't depend on age; it should depend on the individual and other factors, like weight and height. And this should depend on maturity.

I'm way more mature than most thirteen-year-olds and even some twentysomethings. Like Nick.

"What about a private account?" Dana asks.

"If I can only have a private account, then I don't want it at all," I say. "It's completely pointless." My voice gets louder, and a strange burst of anxiety and anger rears up. Suddenly this feels like the most important thing in the world, though I can't explain why. "I have to do this."

Dana shrugs, as if it was never a big deal in the first place. "Okay. Do it."

I sit back, a little deflated at how fast she turned around. "Is it all right if I use the data or do you want me to wait until I can connect to Wi-Fi?"

"Use the data if the signal's strong enough. I'll let you know if we're getting low." We get okay reception here, but if you go back into the canyon beyond the museum, there's basically no service at all.

I pull out my phone and download the app. What should I call my account? I think about being in my yard at night, camping in Hedges, taking photos. Carter told me I can always change the name later. WoodCamera, I try. Someone has that. I add the name of one of my favorite animals: WoodCameraSloth. Bingo. Then, in the description, I write, *I make images of nature with my 4X5 camera.*

No big deal. I look through my camera roll on my phone and select a photo of me with the night sky behind, my face pressed against the telescope. Ezra took that. I'm a little blurry because it's dark, but you can see the sky bright with the constellations. I decide it's fine that nobody can see my face. I'm also wearing a huge jacket so you can't even tell anything about me, except that I'm a human on two legs.

We're eating silently again when I catch Dana giving me a curious stare. I brace myself, thinking she's got bad news, but instead she says, "I saw Ezra's urn was on the table this morning." She swallows some water. "Did you move it?"

Uh-oh. She did notice. I put it back on the mantel as soon as I got home. "Was I not supposed to touch it? I used it for a still life." She doesn't seem mad. Just . . . kind of blank. Her eyes look darker now.

"That's fine. But it's a little odd to take pictures of his urn. Isn't it?" She sprinkles garlic powder on her pizza.

That's exactly what I was afraid of. My shoulders rise as I lower my head. Is she trying to make me feel bad? "I don't know. My art book said to use something that had personal significance."

"You could use the poem," Dana suggests. "Take a photo of that. I don't want you moving the urn."

I don't understand. "Why not?"

"It's not a toy."

"I know it's not a toy. I'm not playing with it." I get up and take the poem out of the urn box. "The paper's tiny, Dana. It didn't work with my composition."

89

She smiles. "Look at you, talking about composition and things."

I reread the poem out loud.

At the place beyond the meadows
On the table where we ate
In white socks we used to roam

I hold up the paper. "This has to mean something. I know Uncle Ezra." I'm more like him than Dana is. Everything he did was deliberate. On purpose.

He always said that sometimes you have to look at things multiple times to understand them. "Things are not always what they seem, Tuesday, in life or in science." He explained that the man who invented the microwave was doing some kind of radar project when the machine he built melted his chocolate bar. The man who discovered penicillin wasn't trying to do that; he was doing some other scientific experiment.

"Uncle Ezra wouldn't write some random thing about white socks into a poem. He'd give it two meanings," I say. I want her to figure this out with me. Talk about it.

Talk about *him*. All the time we spent together. That fun scavenger hunt. The camping.

Hmmm. What else could white socks mean? Is there a literal table? I think of the last time we camped at Hedges with Ezra. We took off our shoes inside the tent and were all wearing white socks, and Ezra made a joke about it. Something like our socks weren't white anymore; they were stained brown with dirt, and there was no point in putting on our shoes if we needed to leave the tent to pee in the middle of the night.

My heart double-thumps. Something like electricity runs over me.

Mesa is Spanish for "table." In geography, a mesa is also a high, flat hill. And we were on a mesa.

Wait.

The last time we went camping, Ezra was joking about being able to find archaeological sites, and he said "maybe he'd already found a site." Dana and I thought he was kidding, but what if he wasn't?

What if he did know something and was going to tell Dana but then got sick and couldn't? And this was his last way of messing with her a little?

That would *so* be an Uncle Ezra thing to do.

I jump up. "Dana! What if these are clues?"

"Clues to what?" She looks at me as if I've grown wings.

I thrust the paper toward her. "What if this is a scavenger hunt? What if it's telling us where an archaeological site is, and each line is a clue? That would be just like Ezra. Remember when we went camping and he said he found a site?"

"He said he *could* find one. And he was joking—trying

to get my goat, as usual." She laughs, then looks sad. "He sure liked doing that."

"What if he wasn't joking?" I sit down. "Dana, if we find a new archaeological site at Hedges, they'll stop construction."

"I know you miss him." Dana wipes her hands. "But this has nothing to do with Hedges. It's a silly little thing he wrote. Maybe it's a riddle, but nothing more. It's not a treasure hunt."

It's not silly. "You're wrong. I think if we could figure out where he means, we'll find something amazing."

Her gaze darkens. "Tuesday . . ."

"I don't understand why you won't even consider it." I stand up so suddenly the chair knocks back. "You know it's the kind of thing he would've done. Found something and then planned to tell you later in some weird, funny way."

"Have you considered the possibility that perhaps you don't get the metaphorical quality of poetry?" Dana asks.

I blink. "What do you mean?"

"I'm saying that you're taking this literally, Tuesday. Poetry is simply not to be taken like a riddle or a mystery novel. It's about feelings. That's all. No scavenger hunt."

My mouth clamps into a line. Anything could be a riddle. Poetry. Science. Art.

It's all about observing it correctly.

I think about how Carter believes what I do, too—that the poem has more meaning. "I have considered that, and I'll tell you that it's wrong."

I can tell Dana's grinding her teeth by how her jaw moves back and forth, trying not to be mad. I speak anyway. "I want to know why you won't even entertain the possibility that I am correct."

Dana laces her hands together. "*I* want to know why you won't take no for an answer."

I don't want to push her, but I don't want to back down, either. What is it with her and Silas avoiding their feelings? And I have to say it's pretty unfair that Dana and other adults have always told me that I should pay more attention to my own feelings. She wants me to be "emotionally intelligent"—able to name what I'm feeling and be aware of other people's emotions. But she's doing the opposite. "Because I am certain I'm correct, Dana."

"Why is this so important to you right now?"

I stare at the floor, at a dust bunny that's rolling lazily along like a desert tumbleweed. Why *is* this important?

Because this Uncle Ezra situation, with the poem and having his ashes here, feels like a rhyme someone stopped reciting in the middle—it needs to be completed. I don't know how to explain this to her. "It just is. You don't want to listen to me."

Dana gets up. "I have to use the restroom. Can you put our plates in the sink?"

I wash the dishes and think about what I need to do. Evidence, I decide. Data. I need more of it so she can't say I'm wrong. Ezra said one of the hardest things about science is staying objective. "We're always looking for the things we wish were there instead of the things that actually are there. You have to be careful," he told me. Dana wishes that Ezra's poem is just a silly thing, so she won't have to deal with it. But it could be more than that. Right? We won't know unless we try.

I just have to get to the mesa.

"Dana," I yell to her, "when are you going to Hedges?"

CHAPTER
12

I get up with the sun and write out in a notebook my action plan for surveying Hedges. Dana's going there in a couple hours. I don't have as much time as I thought I would.

First I copy Ezra's poem.

At the place beyond the meadows
On the table where we ate
In white socks we used to roam

I chew on my pen and think.

Possible meanings of white socks:
-The literal white socks we wear
-The baseball team (unlikely)

Time for the next step. I get out Dana's *Archaeological Compliance Guidance* copy—a sixty-five-page document. It tells you how to get permits and look for archaeological sites. One section is called "Intensive Pedestrian Survey," which is what I'm going to do. Basically, you have to make a line that's about fifty feet long (which is fifteen meters) along where you're looking and mark when you find things with a little flag. You could do this with spray paint, but I don't want to damage the environment. Dana's got a roll of thick white string, so I dig that out. Since I don't have actual flags, I'll use sticks. I jot down:

Hike to where we camped
Mark off the line
Find what Uncle Ezra was talking about

The mesa isn't that big. I can survey the whole thing in an afternoon. And maybe once I'm back there, with his poem, I'll be able to figure out the clues.

"Ready, Tuesday?" Dana calls.

I shove the supplies into my backpack and grab my camera stuff. "Ready."

Dana and I drive to Hedges. One thing most people don't know about Zion is that it's full of ancient archaeological sites, but they have different levels of secrecy. One level is open to the public. Another level is the "if they ask, then tell" level, where if someone specifically asks about how to get to a site, the rangers are allowed to tell them. And the final level is total secrecy, which basically only Dana's team knows where it is.

Dana's current project, of course, is to look at the Mormon dwellings. "It's not well studied," Dana says, "because there are more ancient sites that get more interest." The Mormons started settling around here in 1862—which is the year before the Emancipation Proclamation. Dana's found several of these sites, but my mission—which I'm not telling her about yet—is to find a different, new site. The one Ezra said he found.

Dana's telling me about how many of the Mormon settlers kept journals, but there was a Native American point of view that's not documented. Because one historical fact that most people don't know is that some Mormons had Paiute slaves. When I went to regular school here, the history books didn't mention it. I only know because of Dana. And just because slavery got outlawed doesn't mean everything was completely fair after that.

Some of the journals talk about how they "bought" the land in Hedges from a Paiute man. "But then he came back and built a house on the land they thought they bought—and it seems like they left him alone." Dana shakes her head. "But that's only one point of view. It's possible that this man thought the Mormons wanted to live there for one season, which would make sense to him, because the Native Americans moved around during the year, following the animals." Dana could talk for hours on this subject.

I know why the school history books don't say anything about it. They don't want people to feel bad about what their ancestors did. But just because someone doesn't want to know a fact, or doesn't like a fact, doesn't mean the fact doesn't exist anymore. It's like not wanting to know that it's over a hundred degrees today—you may not like the temperature, but if you accept it, you can do the right things, like take extra water with you.

Not knowing facts always leads to trouble.

Dana grumbles about the crowds as we exit the park. "It gets worse every year. And it's even worse because of that Lyla Redding person."

"That's what I was afraid of when she visited," I say. She may be a conservationist, but she didn't help preserve this park by showing up here and advertising it. I open Instagram. Carter's followed her with our account. She's posted the pictures her team took of Zion. They're mostly of her posing dramatically in front of the cliffs. They look almost small behind her. *Giant*, I type, and to my surprise she hearts it immediately. Or probably her assistant hearts it.

There's one photo of her with the falcon, Alice. She's squatting beside the cage, the door open so you can see the bird. Lyla's posted the fact about it being the fastest animal and also has links to donate to the Audubon Society and wildlife rescues.

We enter the ranch property. The lady on the trail said they'd started construction, and indeed there's a bunch of construction equipment here at the front. A woman operating a backhoe is digging up the vineyard, the grapevines getting crushed and sending clouds of splinters into the air.

Dana sighs. "I hear those grapes were spotty anyway. They stopped taking care of them ages ago."

My insides tense up. "Why didn't the family leave the ranch to the park?" I ask. "Or why couldn't someone buy it and leave it to the park?"

"That was explored," Dana says. "Back before Julie was superintendent, the old superintendent turned down an offer. The park doesn't have the resources to take care of so much additional land. We don't have the funding."

"Couldn't we get more funding?" To be honest, I'm not sure how funding works. Even though the adults talk about it all the time.

"That's not how the government works," Dana replies. "Remember how they shut down the federal government a few times? That includes these parks, and it was a disaster for a lot of them. Like Joshua Tree in California—people came in and destroyed the trees and left trash everywhere." She shakes her head. "We don't have enough money or staff to handle the amount of people we get now."

I understand what she means. Everyone who works at Zion wanted to limit the number of people who come in every day—like some other national parks do—but the Utah lawmakers and the governor all said no. They said the state depends on the money that Zion makes for them. Dana's been complaining about that the whole time she's been here.

"If the state wants you to take in more people," I say, "then they should give you more money, too." I think of the crowds now and how there will be even more when Hedges is done. "Pretty soon there's not going to be a park to visit."

Dana thumps her hands on the steering wheel. "Exactly, Tuesday. It seems like everyone knows that except the people who actually give us money to run it."

I look out the window, a frown making my forehead hurt. Why can't people do sensible things? Why can't the public take care of the parks, even if there are no rangers there to tell them not to destroy the landscape? I hope it gets fixed before I'm completely grown up. Otherwise, I might have to run for some kind of office so I can fix it all, which I would hate since I don't really like talking to people. But I would do it if I had to.

CHAPTER

13

We go farther into the canyon, where the public's not allowed, past burned-out wooden buildings and some sheds that make it look like a small ghost town. It's pretty cool to get to see this, or so Dana tells me.

Over here is where the settlers cleared land and basically turned it into a prairie for their cattle or whatever. Some domestic sheep wander around in the distance. "Have those sheep been here forever?"

"For a good while," Dana says. "There's plenty to eat here."

Beyond this prairie is where the land is pristine. That's where the other sites probably are, if they exist. Including the one I think Ezra found.

Dana's survey handbook says that if a construction crew finds something archaeological, work must stop immediately within a fifty-foot radius. I bet they'll stop beyond that—fifty feet isn't much.

I've got a notebook, a pen, my phone, my water, and my camera stuff. I'm going to tell Dana I want to take photos—and that's when I'll look for new archaeological sites. My stomach is a little nervous, as if I'm hiding something. But I'm not. Surveying is just like walking around. It's not like I'm planning to rappel off a cliff or ride a canoe down the river alone.

Out on the dig, there are a bunch of seasonal archaeology interns who are here on a grant through a university, but they're from all over. Cass, Dante, and Na. From San Diego, Michigan, and New Hampshire. They're on their hands and knees, digging around very slowly. Which means they're doing more scraping than digging.

The thing about the soil here is it's very sandy. That means that lots of items got preserved because they sort of fell into the soil, and it's like finding toys in a sandbox. In other parts of the country, the soil's hard, so there aren't as many finds.

I know all this because I've been coming on digs with my mother since I was a baby strapped to her chest. I admit that I've complained about it, but I still picked up a ton of information against my will. Now that I'm old enough to feed myself, I mostly stay out of the digs unless it's interesting.

Or unless I want to do something else near the site.

Na tells me to look at sand in a sieve. "I already gave

it the once-over," she says, "but make sure I didn't miss anything. Use your young eyes."

"My eyes aren't that much younger. You're like twenty-one."

"Still. I kind of ruined them with my phone." She pushes her glasses up her nose. "Your mom's doing you a favor by being old-school."

"How do you know about that?"

Na shrugs. "Dana talks."

I wonder what else Dana has told them about me. Hopefully not that they have to watch me today. I look through the sand and find a tiny sliver of pottery, blue and white, different from the stones. It's easy to miss because the edges are smooth and rounded like a pebble, but it's definitely not one. I point it out to Na, and she plucks it out with tweezers and puts it into a baggie.

This is not what I want to be doing, though. I want to start my survey of where we camped. Where Ezra might have found something.

I need to think of an excuse to get away from the group so I can start my survey. And I don't want to raise Dana's suspicions. It's like eating a cookie before dinner. If she sees me doing it, because she's supposed to be a parent, she will tell me not to. If she doesn't see me doing it and I still eat my vegetables, then she won't care if I ate a cookie, even if I tell her later.

Therefore, my plan is to take some photos and look

for sites at the same time. That way, if Dana asks what I'm doing, I can honestly say I'm taking photos. And I do actually want to take photos.

The seasonals are talking about the ranch sale. "They can't just close this down." Dante gulps some water. "It's historic."

"They'll cordon off this part." Cass pushes her floppy hat back. Her eyes are a bright blue. "Maybe they'll make it part of a park or something."

"I would totally buy a house here." Na shades her eyes, gazing out at the landscape. She's wearing bright blue eyeliner that matches a blue streak in her hair. "Especially if there's actually some cool stores."

Everyone looks at her.

"What?" she says. "I'm an archaeologist, not an environmentalist."

"Shame," Dante says, and sprays her with his water bottle. Na shrieks, then sprays him back, and they giggle as they squirt each other. I watch silently. They're acting like they're five. I want to point out to Dana how mature I am compared to them—maybe then she won't tell anyone to keep an eye on me—but she's occupied in the other corner of the dig site, her laptop out.

"Ugh. Don't get me wet." I shield my camera with my body.

Na pauses the water fight. "What is that thing, anyway?"

"A camera."

"Get any good photos? I want to see. Do you have an Instagram?" Dante takes out his phone, ready to type.

"As a matter of fact, I do." Carter was right. I tell him my handle, and they all add me.

"How do you have ten thousand followers, Dante?" Na asks.

He shrugs. "I have a very strong meme game."

"Love the camera. Old-school," Cass says. "Very cool."

"That rhymes." Na makes muscles with her biceps. "Do you want a photo of me? In case I'm the next Indiana Jones."

"You can't be a fictional character, Na," Cass says.

"Besides which, Indiana Jones was the worst archaeologist ever. He ignored all the rules. He stole artifacts belonging to other cultures. And he was afraid of snakes." Dante puts down his shovel and lists all of Indiana Jones's travesties on his gloved fingers. "Heck, I see three snakes a day out here. He would have never made it in the field."

"But he was a genius with the whip," Na says.

Dana's still occupied. This is my chance. "Hey, I'm going to walk around and take some photos. I'll be back in an hour."

"Yeah, sure. I'll tell Dana," Cass says. "If you can't hear us, you've gone too far."

"I know." I know all these things. Dana and Ezra

have fully prepared me for survival. If I got lost out here, I could survive a week, easily. I've got a whistle around my neck. In my backpack, I have a folded light jacket and a flint starter—that's a piece of magnesium with a striking device—so I can make a fire. Ezra gave me a Leatherman for my tenth birthday, which is in the side pouch of my backpack. It has a knife and screwdriver and all sorts of useful tools on it. And he showed me which cacti are edible. My CamelBak holds three liters of water, which weighs more than six and a half pounds.

I don't point any of this out to the seasonals.

I walk away from the site, down the riverbank, taking care not to crush plants. But what does it matter if that backhoe is going to scoop up everything, anyway?

I round a corner and stop.

The river continues ahead of me. To my left, there's a smaller offshoot that goes into a slot canyon—which is a narrower version of the main canyon, with walls so tall it throws the path into shade. Slot canyons are where you have to be careful, because if there's a flash flood, there's nowhere to go. Some of them are only a few feet wide and a thousand feet tall, and there's not even a riverbank to stand on. However, today's weather is completely clear.

I enter a slot canyon about ten feet wide that forks in a few directions, heading up to the campsite where I hope to find what Uncle Ezra was talking about in his poem. Sunlight slants in, making everything too bright. This canyon runs east to west. The Zion canyon runs north to south. That means this canyon gets plenty of light. Which means it was easier to grow things. These are all things Dana told me. Of course people mostly chose to live here. They went into Zion canyon sometimes to forage or, in the way-back times, to fish when it was a lake.

In Zion, people would get down into the canyon by ladders tied to holds on the rocks. I look up, searching for any of those. I'm not sure if there are any still here. It's hard to tell now if something is carved in there and what's an indentation because it's all been worn away. Plus it's probably too high up for me to see.

As I walk, the canyon opens up to fifty, then a hundred feet wide. Now there's river rock in the middle, then random sharp-edged stones, then a sandy bank, then actual regular land. I see a craggy tower with lots of shadows and shapes above. It's a hoodoo. If you've ever taken wet sand and piled it up, that's what it looks like. It also looks like a cave stalagmite, except it's outside and has more textures to it, because of the wind hitting it all the time. It's about thirty feet tall.

I set up the camera, trying to compose the shot like I saw in the art book. I draw the frame into thirds in my head and take the photo.

Then I continue along the slot canyon path, my feet

sinking into the sand, which is more like large pebbles than the fine sand at a beach. This is on the way to our secret camping area. There wouldn't be any archaeological sites here—the water washes everything away, and it's not where we camped. The canyon forks again, and I take the path to the left and follow the steep trail up out of the canyon, emerging into a wide, flat area—our secret mesa.

It's a prairie grassland, a meadow bordered with cottonwood trees, continuing on for a distance before another slot canyon entrance appears. Birds sing, and the wind blows through the grasses with a *shooshing* noise.

I pant for a few minutes, though the hike wasn't as hard as I remembered. I am a little bigger than I was last year, so maybe that's why it's easier. There's the small, mostly dirt clearing where we put up our tent and made our campfire; we completely cleaned it up the next day. All that's left is a few pieces of burnt wood.

One of the cottonwood trees bows over a fallen tree in an interesting, curved way that reminds me of a ballerina's arm, the sky beyond it. I set up the tripod on a flat area of dry grass among a bunch of old branches. Then I put the cape over my head, turn the focus knob until the upside-down image sharpens, and finally squeeze the bulb on the cord. The shutter clicks in a loud, mechanical, satisfying way.

I take my hat off and wipe my sweaty head. This area will be impossible for me to examine easily, because it's all covered with fallen branches, bark, and cottonwood leaves. There are small holes here and there, animal burrows that probably belong to squirrels and rabbits.

In white socks we used to roam.

This is it. Where we used to roam. Where Ezra was talking about finding a new site. I'll start making my line at the firepit campsite. I tie a piece of string to a stick and put that in the ground. It's hard to get it in there, because the earth is so dry and packed. The stick only goes in a little bit and is at a weird angle. Then I unwind my string, walking slowly along, poking under the stuff on the ground. I don't have any way to measure fifty feet, so I count to fifty, then stop.

There's absolutely nothing.

I do it twice more, and then I run out of string. Whoops. I grit my teeth, frustrated. "Why couldn't you tell us where there was a site?" I ask the air. "Why do you have to make things hard?"

"They're not hard, they're interesting," I can hear Uncle Ezra respond.

My legs and back ache from the hike and bending over to mess with the string. This was not easy work. I sit cross-legged on the ground, letting the breeze dry off my sweaty self, and eat an apple, listening to—well, nothing. For a second, the chatter in my head goes away, and I'm not thinking about archaeology or photography or Ezra or how Dana is going to move us or how Carter's leaving me on my own.

I didn't know my own head was so noisy. And then I realize something.

I can't hear anyone from the site.

I'm ridiculously far away. I should go back. Maybe Dana hasn't noticed yet. I take out my phone.

Oops. I've been gone for more than two hours.

I fold up the tripod and load up my stuff and head back down the way I came, walking at a fast shuffle through the sand pebbles, my breath and my feet noisy in the quiet air. The tripod falls off my shoulder, and I shrug it back on.

As I get to the fork, I hear Dana shouting, "Tuesday! TUESDAY!"

I begin running clumsily with my equipment. I think about using my whistle, but then my mother will think I'm in danger. "Dana!" I yell. "Coming!"

I take the fork in the slot canyon and almost bump into her around the corner. As expected, she looks less than pleased. "What are you doing all the way back here alone?"

"Taking photos of where we went camping." This is the truth. The archaeology thing did not go anywhere. I clench my jaw, frustrated, thinking about Ezra's poem. If this wasn't the place, then where is it?

"I thought I could trust your judgment." Dana shakes her head. Her face is red and sweaty, her shirt is sticking to her, and I realize she probably ran all the way here, looking for me. "I won't bring you anymore if you're going to wander off."

"I didn't wander off. I told you, I was doing something important."

Her mouth tenses into a line. "I yelled for you, and you didn't answer. You're not supposed to go beyond—"

"What I can hear." I roll my eyes. "I am not a dog on a leash. I'm a perfectly capable person."

"You're twelve." Dana starts walking back.

That is a fact. I don't know why she brings it up, though—I'm twelve, but that doesn't mean I don't understand things. "Irrelevant," I mutter, and she doesn't stop, but I know she hears because she walks faster. "Look, Dana, there's nobody back here. The worst thing that could happen is I step on a rattlesnake, and you know I look out for those."

"You could've fallen down a cliff and died."

"I could also fall down at home," I point out. "Most fatal accidents take place where you live, not outside."

She shakes her head. "No coming back here alone. Ever. Understand?"

"Yeah," I mutter.

"This is serious. Say it so I can hear you."

"YES!" I shout. "Yes. I won't come back here alone. I

understand you think I'm a helpless little kid. Okay?"

She closes her eyes and takes a few breaths. That probably made her even angrier, but I don't care. Dana turns, gesturing at me as she does. "Okay. Come on. I have to get back to work."

Now I'm doubly glad I didn't tell her about the archaeology search, because she'd probably get mad about me not having permits. Not that I could get permits.

I trudge behind her, letting Dana get far enough ahead of me that I can see her but still be kind of far away. I wonder if she'll turn around to check if I'm still there.

She doesn't look back once.

CHAPTER
14

The next day around noon, Dana drives me into town to meet Silas at the photographer. Carter went to St. George with Jenny to do some shopping, and I wish I could wait for him. I don't even really want to go. I want to return to Hedges and look for sites again. But I know Dana's still a little mad at me for wandering off and there's no way she's going to take me.

I'll have to think of a new angle. I just don't know what it is yet.

We pass Hedges, the construction equipment all roaring away, and I turn my head so I don't have to see it. I am failing Uncle Ezra.

"Look for Tootsie's Diner," Dana says. "It's behind that."

I know where that is, but we've only eaten there maybe once. I never noticed a photography studio nearby. We've never needed to go to one.

We pass the turn for the library, then some other tourist stuff, and I see the sign for Tootsie's, written in white cursive on wood. "There!"

We make a sharp right into a small parking lot, then down a little unpaved road to a small building. A wooden sign with purple cursive letters says *Dover Photography*.

I've never noticed that sign before or the building in the back. You can drive by things a hundred times if you aren't paying attention. I guess you have to *want* to be paying attention before you see things sometimes.

We go inside. A little bell dings when the door opens.

"Be right there!" a woman's voice calls out.

This room is a small gallery with a low ceiling and windows at the short end of the long rectangle. Framed photos of the park hang in both black and white and color, all matted with white paper and hung in black frames. One wall is covered with nothing but night sky photos, and I zoom over to that one. I already know from astronomy that digital cameras pick up more starlight than the naked eye.

One of the photographs makes me freeze. It's of Watchman with a meteor shower behind it.

It reminds me of the time I went to Hedges with Uncle Ezra, and we watched a meteor shower. "Did you know," he'd said, "we're descended from stars? Most of the elements in the human body were made in a star. But first it starts small, with water and air. It's galactic chemical evolution."

"What about when we die?" I'd asked.

"We break down and become part of the earth again," he said. "It's comforting."

Then we sat on our blanket and drank hot chocolate, watching the meteors burn their way to Earth.

The door jingles, and Silas comes in. "Hi, you must be Dana. Good to meet you." He shakes Dana's hand, and they have some boring adult small talk. "I can give her a ride back, if that's okay," he says. "I have to do a lecture at the museum anyway."

"Thank you so much." Dana looks at me. "You okay if I go?"

I nod, and my mother leaves.

These prints are pretty spectacular. There's a photo of the night sky, with stars that leave trails, so many that it looks swirled, like a painting I've seen before. One that's always being reproduced on posters and coffee mugs. "Van Gogh's *Starry Night!*" I say out loud.

"Indeed." Silas says. "Do you know why there are trails of light like that?"

I shake my head.

"You have to put the camera on a slow shutter setting, because it's dark and that lets enough light into the photo. But the shutter doesn't move fast enough to capture the movement, so it looks like the stars are leaving a trail," Silas explains.

That is something I did not know. Before I have a chance to keep asking Silas questions, a door into the back opens and a woman enters, blinking as if the light hurts her eyes.

"I thought I heard the bell! Hello! You must be Silas and Tuesday. I'm Danielle." She has short gray hair that's a little bit curly. Her mouth and eyes crinkle when she smiles. I have no idea how old she is, but I'm guessing grandmother age. She's wearing a heavy-duty black plastic apron, I guess to keep chemicals from splashing all over her and her clothes.

"Guilty as charged." Silas shakes her hand. He tells almost as many dad jokes as Grant.

Danielle laughs at that. "How's your residency going? Is it hard to be away from your regular life in the middle of nowhere?"

Silas hesitates, and he gets that same odd look as he had when we were at his cabin asking about photographs. "It's all right."

"We're not really in the middle of nowhere." I kind of hate it when people say that. "We can still get cell signal sometimes, and there's indoor plumbing." To me the middle of nowhere means you backpack to a place with your sleeping bag, and if you poop, you have to poop in a bag and carry it back out or bury it.

"That's true," Silas says. "It's a once-in-a-lifetime experience to be here."

"Great." Danielle claps her hands. "Let's get you set up."

"Thank you for doing this," Silas says. "I felt bad when I realized Tuesday had no way of developing the film."

"My pleasure. I've been meaning to work with young artists."

We follow Danielle into a back room through the door she came in. The room is dark, lit by a red light bulb so it looks like a horror movie. The chemical smell is strong and reminds me of a beauty parlor. As my eyes adjust, I decide it used to be a kitchen with lots of cabinets and counters.

Shallow plastic tubs sit on a counter next to a sink, and above the opposite counter there's a clothesline with wet photographs dripping into more tubs. "You have to keep the light out or it will ruin the photos," she says. "Get your film."

I remove the film from the protective covers. Danielle takes a large canister and shows me how to set the film in there, carefully curved. "Developer time," she says, and fills up the canister. "Leave it for about ten minutes. It's so wonderful that you're using a four-by-five camera," Danielle says. "The old methods are making a comeback."

"For sure," Silas says. "A lot of my college students are all about using real film."

"And listening to vinyl records," Danielle adds. "It's like going back to my youth in the seventies. How did you get into photography, Tuesday?"

"Silas threw away his camera," I inform Danielle. "I'm using it now."

Danielle gives Silas the same look Carter gave me when I turned down Oreos, his favorite snack, for the first time. "Why's that? You don't do photography anymore?"

Silas isn't looking at us, his face turned away in the semidarkness. "Nope. Too many bad memories."

Danielle nods. "I get that. After my husband passed away, I couldn't even look at a camera for a year because that's what we used to do together." Danielle adds another liquid to the canister. "This is stop bath."

"That stops the photos from overdeveloping," Silas says.

I'm confused. "Did you have bad memories because of your husband, or good?"

Danielle gives me a thoughtful look. "Painful is a more accurate word," she says. "And even ten years later, it can still be painful sometimes." She sighs. "Grief is a funny thing. It's not an event with a beginning and an end. It can pop up again. We were married for more than thirty years, after all."

My heart double-thumps. Does this mean I'll always be sad about Uncle Ezra? I didn't ever think about that before. I thought my sadness would stop, sooner or later. Run out the same way a boiling pot of water runs out. "Do you ever stop missing him?"

"No. But you get used to it. And what I like to do is pretend he's gone on a trip, and I can't talk to him right now." She smiles, though her eyes turn down, and my throat closes. Does that mean that Dana will always be like this about Ezra?

Silas has turned around and is listening intently, his eyes a little watery. "You must be glad you had so much time together. That you didn't waste it."

"Yes. Life isn't for wasting." She tilts her head at him. "Or regrets."

Silas nods. I wonder what his whole story is. I decide not to ask. He'll share when he's ready, I guess.

"And finally, fixer. This gets rid of some other chemicals and allows the film to be exposed to light safely." Danielle unrolls the film from the canister and holds it against the red light bulb. "Voilà! Images."

Science at work again.

I peer at the film. Yes, there's the view of Watchman, with the boulder. "Well, that's sort of magical, isn't it?"

"Magical indeed," Silas says, and he sounds happier than I've ever heard him.

After the negatives are dry, we put each one into the enlarger and make a proof sheet. You put a piece of photo paper under the enlarger and turn on the light so it shines through the negative. Then you take the paper and put it into a developer bath—which is what the shallow pans are for—and the image shows up.

Two four-by-five images fit on each sheet of paper. "That way we don't have to enlarge all the photos in case you don't like them." When they're done developing, Silas clips them to a line over the sink, and we turn on the lights to look at them.

"Who says you're not an artist?" Danielle says to me. "Look at the composition on this one. We should enlarge it." She points to the boulder.

"That was my friend Carter's idea." I feel another pang of guilt for not waiting for Carter. Basically, he made that photo. He should be here. "Is it okay if I come back and bring my friend?"

"Of course."

Silas gestures at the image of the urn and telescope. "What's in the box?"

For a second, I remember what Dana said about it being weird to mess with the urn. I consider lying. But Silas already thinks I'm strange, so what does it matter? "My uncle's ashes."

Both he and Danielle jump a little, as if I've handed them a hot potato. "They're important to you," Silas says, and I'm glad he doesn't sound weirded out.

"I get it." Danielle smiles at me kindly. "I had my

husband's ashes on my bedside table for a long time, before I hiked up to his final resting place." She shakes her head. "He wanted me to keep going with my life, so he told me to put them on Mount Rainier. I had to work out for six months to be able to get halfway up!"

"Did he tell you that before he died?" I ask.

"He wrote it in a note," she answers. "A silly little rhyme. '*Roses are red, violets are blue. Put my ashes on Mount Rainier or I'll always haunt you!*'" She chuckles. "He had a dark sense of humor."

"My kind of person." Silas grins. "Want to make an eight by ten, Tuesday?"

"Sure," I say. "Let's do the boulder."

They show me how to use the enlarger to shine a light through the negative onto the print paper, then put it in each chemical bath. Finally, we hang it up on a string over the sink. I turn to Silas. "Can I develop the photos from Hedges?"

He looks at his phone. "Another day, okay? I have to get back and do a lecture."

I shrug. I want to bring Carter back anyway. And they're not really so important since I didn't even find any archaeology, are they? "Another day."

CHAPTER

15

anielle gives me some negatives she says are "gathering dust" and then Silas drops me at Dana's office, and I hang out in there using the Wi-Fi while she works. I take a photo of the boulder print and upload it to Instagram. *Did you know that Zion was once an ocean, and after that was a desert? That's where the sandstone came from,* I type. *Never try to move boulders or write on them. You're ruining millions of years of development.* I wrote that because people think that stacking rocks to make art is fun, but it messes with the environment—too many rocks end up getting moved around.

"Grant says you're going rock climbing with him and Carter tomorrow," Dana says. "I said that didn't sound like you."

"It's true." I'm lying on a beanbag chair, looking up at the ceiling and listening to Dana clacking away on her keyboard. I want to go because Carter wants me to, but I also don't want to because, well, I'm not good with heights. "Maybe I should cancel."

"It's up to you," Dana says. "The route Grant's going to take is pretty interesting, though. It's in a little canyon offshoot on the east side that's technically part of Hedges. Pretty much a secret area."

I sit up so fast my spine cracks. "Really?"

What? This bit of information makes up my mind for real. "Do you think there are any archaeological sites over there? Maybe places where people stored food in the cliffs or caves or something?" Along the scenic road in the park, there's a site like that, built under a sandstone overhang.

"Anything's possible," Dana answers.

"I think I'll go," I say as casually as possible. "Try it out." See if I can find something that will stop the development.

"If you want to." She grins at me. "Let me know if you find any signs that people lived there."

I smile back at her. Dana pretty much just gave me the okay to survey this area. This is going to be great. Of course, it's nowhere near the spot we camped, but if there was another archaeological site, it could at least stop construction for a while until it got investigated.

I look up at her bookcase. It's filled with rows and rows of archaeology books. I search for one about the Paiute living here.

Dana's stuck a bunch of framed family photos in front of the books, so many they overlap. There are her parents. Me as a baby. Me as a second grader, missing teeth. Me, her, and Ezra. Lots more of me. One of two little kids I don't recognize, with a sort of golden haze over it like the colors ran together. This one is partially hidden behind a photo of me and Ezra with his telescope. I sit up and scoot closer, taking out the one of the kids.

The two kids stand in a field with a tent behind them. Now I can see that it's not a sunset filter, it was taken in the 1980s, when film looked like that, and that the two kids are Dana and Ezra. I'd know Ezra by his cheesy, too-wide grin anywhere, his head thrown back, his dark hair in a shaggy bowl cut, his skinny legs with striped ankle socks and hiking boots. I do look like Ezra, I see. Dana looks like a smaller version of herself, serious-faced, looking into the camera as if she's solving a math problem.

Ezra's holding a black-and-white cat on a leash. That's unusual, but maybe not that unusual for someone like Ezra.

I sneeze. The photo's dusty.

"Gesundheit!" Dana thrusts a box of tissues at me.

"Thanks." I pull one out, blow my nose. "What's up with you and Ezra and this cat?"

"We used to take the cat camping. He was more like a dog than a cat. He went everywhere with us." Dana chuckles. "Plus, you know Ezra liked to do odd things like take a cat camping, just to show it could be done." The clacking resumes.

I almost can't believe it—she's not ignoring the subject of Ezra. I take out another tissue and carefully wipe the dust off the photo. "Did you go camping a lot?" The book I need turns out to be behind that photo. I take it out.

"As much as we could. My mom liked fishing, so if there was good fishing nearby, we could talk them into going anywhere."

"Did Ezra like fishing?" He'd never taken me, never mentioned it.

"Not so much. It took too much time. He didn't like to be that still for long."

That sounds like Ezra. I smile at the young Ezra and put the frame back in the bookcase so it's in front of the photo of me. "Ezra would have hated what's happening with Hedges."

"Yeah. But sometimes bad things happen, Tuesday, and there's not a thing anyone can do about them. No sense in making yourself worried over things you can't control." Her tone means *this is the end of it.* I've learned to recognize that tone—it means I'd better drop whatever I was talking about.

I bristle and ignore her tone on purpose. "Is it something we can't control?"

"Yes. Working in government, that's the first thing you learn. Don't let the bureaucrats drive you into the ground." She sighs out a breath. "You can go on home if you want. This report is taking longer than I thought."

I think she's just tired of me asking questions. But fine. Maybe she does have to finish the report, and it must be hard to do that while you're also watching a kid. Even though I require no watching. "Okay. The couch is more comfortable to lie on anyway." I get up and gather my stuff.

"I'll be home in two hours," Dana says, without looking up from her computer.

"Yup." I hold up the book. "I'm going to take this for research."

She waves at me. I leave before I can wonder any more about what Dana's feeling, or why every conversation I have with her seems so hard these days.

CHAPTER
16

In the morning, Delilah comes roaring up, and Grant, Carter, and I head over to the east side. I'm trying to give myself a pep talk. I still don't really want to boulder, but I have to. What if this area has some archaeological site, or a clue of some kind that'll lead to one?

Besides, Carter asked me to, and he's never asked me before. I'm nervous, but I tell myself that climbing with Grant and Carter is actually safer than learning how to do this in a class with twenty kids in it, because the instructor to student ratio is better. I can't die. Well, I guess I could, but the possibility is very low. Mathematically, that is. I jiggle my leg anxiously as Delilah drives up the road toward Hedges.

"What are you thinking about?" Carter asks.

I don't tell him about the internal monologue I just had. "Nothing."

Grant drives us up route 9 to the east side. There, he pulls off the road, making sure Delilah's off the pavement. I get out of the car and retrieve my gear. We're parked by what looks like a rolling hillside of pinkish boulders, spotted with the occasional pine tree. At the bottom, the ground is all pinkish-tan sandy dirt. But there's no trail marker. "Where are we going, exactly? There's no trailhead."

"It's unmarked, because we don't want people to know about this place." Grant takes out a crash pad, which looks like a thick, folded up mat you'd use for gymnastics. He wiggles his brows at me. "Top secret. And no going back here without an adult," he says to Carter.

Carter laughs. "I would have to steal Delilah and drive back here. It's a long hike, all uphill." Nobody can walk up the highway on foot—they'd get smooshed by a car.

I put on my super-big hat with the long flaps on the sides and back, then strap on my CamelBak, then put the tripod and camera on, too. Good thing I'm strong. I follow Grant and Carter across the dirt, which is almost like a beach except there's no water.

One of the boulders is really more like a small hill made of rock, with ridges worn into it by sun and rain, making nice little foot ledges. Grant walks up this diagonally. Carter waits for me. "Doing okay?"

"We've been walking for literally thirty seconds." I adjust the CamelBak. "I'm fine."

We walk up the boulder-hill and over the crest. I glance back at the car—it seems very far down all of a sudden. We're like thirty feet up from the road. The incline was so gentle I didn't notice we were getting higher.

On the other side is a sort of shallow canyon made of rock. Grant leads us in a zigzag pattern down the steep sandstone, my hiking boots gripping the orange-brown ridges. I follow blindly, taking sips of water. It takes a long time, and sometimes I'm pretty much on my bottom, holding on to the rocks with my hands.

When we get to the valley floor, I glance back and can't really tell where the trail is. I hope nothing happens to Grant and Carter, not only because they're my friends but because I'd be lost. Amateur move. I concentrate on finding a landmark—there's a gnarled gray dead piñon—and decide to remember that.

Now that we're inside the canyon, there's two ways to go—left or right—along a dry riverbed covered in loose, round stones. "Left is the way," Grant says, and we follow him along the dry riverbank. The ground turns to beachy sand here, very loose and hard to walk in. The stones wobble too much, so I go back to following Carter.

We're in a slot canyon, a narrow opening in the rocky mountain. Above us on both sides, sandstone cliffs rise high into the sky, pockmarked with countless holes and ridges carved over thousands of years.

I scan the sky for clouds—it's blue and dotted with fat squat cotton-ball ones. You always want to watch for rain here.

I've been in canyons like this lots of times. You get used to seeing them, the way you get used to seeing the houses on your block. But today, after trying photography, I find myself noticing how the holes in the rock cast shadows on the canyon wall, the fine texture of the sand as my mud-caked boots crunch into it, and wondering how this will all look in black and white.

We seem to be going deeper into the earth, the sky getting farther and farther away, the air growing colder as the walls cast a deeper shadow over us. I look for signs that humans were ever here—maybe hand and footholds carved into the walls. A hollowed-out little spot for food storage. Anything. It looks completely pristine, though. "Where are we?" I ask.

"We've come down into Parunuweap Canyon," Grant answers. He's eyeing a reddish-brown cliff above us. There's a cave at the top, about twelve feet up—the wind has hollowed out lots of different spaces in the sandstone. "And now we're in Hedges."

Hedges. I whisper to Carter, "Keep an eye out for any archaeology, okay?"

"Okay," Carter whispers back.

Grant sets the crash pad down and gets out a helmet and a pair of climbing shoes, then hands them to me. "This is one of the easiest beginner routes I've found."

"I'd like to know what your definition of *beginner* is, then," I say to him. I look up at the sandstone wall. It's got an interesting texture, with shadows where the sun hits the crevices and dips, and I set up my tripod and camera.

Maybe there's an archaeological area inside that cave. "Has this area been surveyed?"

"It's been surveyed for animals," Grant says. "Not for archaeology."

"Carter," I say. "Go up there and see if there are any signs that people used it."

"I don't know what to look for," Carter says.

"Smoke-stained ceiling. Places where they hollowed out the wall to store stuff."

"Maybe. But I probably would've noticed that before," Grant says. "Then again, I wasn't looking."

That means it's possible. "You can do it, Carter," I say to him. "I'll stay here and take photos."

"We brought you shoes," Carter says. "Climb up with me. You're the one who can find archaeological stuff."

I take in a deep breath and peer up at the wall. He's probably right. Only one of us has a parent who's taken them on digs for twelve years. If anyone can find evidence that people lived here, it's me. "Okay." I sit down, taking off my boots and socks and putting on the shoes. These have sticky rubber toes—and they're incredibly stinky. "Phew!" I wave my hand at them but have no choice but to put them on. These used to be Carter's, obviously. "My toes are squished."

"They're supposed to be tight. Helps your toes grip better." Carter pushes on the end with his fingers.

Grant sticks the helmet on my head. Carter's already put his on. "Carter, you want to explain how to fall?"

"How to fall?" I squeak. This doesn't sound good. "I don't want to fall at all. Let's skip that lesson."

"Nobody wants to fall." Carter sticks his hands into a small cylindrical bag that has a drawstring on top. "But it happens. So you have to know what to do." His hands come out covered in white powder. Chalk dust—it's to make his grip better. He clambers up. He seems to know where to put his hands and feet, balanced on the little spots that jut out or gripping the crevices. "You want to land in a squatting position and let yourself roll." Carter drops down onto the crash pad and does just that.

"It's like being a cat," Grant says. "Don't try to fight it. But draw your hands up next to you and tuck your chin." Grant demonstrates.

That's a lot to remember. It's easier for me to remember lists if they don't involve me actually doing the body work. I'm a little awkward with most physical activities, which is why you won't see me dancing or bike riding.

They make me climb up a foot or so. "Have three points of contact at all times," Grant says and shows me where to start with my feet and hands. "Now move one hand up. Then one foot."

I move myself maybe a half an inch.

"Perfect," Grant says. "Now fall."

I let go, trying to imitate Carter's stance. I forget to tuck my head, and when I land, I immediately fall to the side, and even though my hand feels like it wants to stop my movement I won't let it.

"Good job, Tuesday!" Grant pats my back. "But tuck your chin down next time." He points at the wall. "One more time."

"Are you joking?"

"Not about safety." Grant gives me a serious look. "Go on."

Reluctantly I climb up again. It's easier this time and I go higher than I had before—probably five feet. "Can I jump down from this height?" I'm a little scared.

"You're fine," Grant says.

I have no choice. So I let go, tuck my chin, and roll. I hit the crash pad hard, and it doesn't hurt but it's shocking.

"Great job!" Grant helps me up.

My heart's racing like I ran a marathon. "Yeah. I don't want to do that ever again." Archaeological site or no archaeological site. I just can't do this like a frog can't grow wings and fly. I take off my helmet and wipe my forehead. "I'm done."

"You haven't even gotten started!" Carter says. "What's the point of coming all the way out here if you won't even try?"

"Carter, it's okay. Tuesday just needs a break," Grant says.

I shake my head. "I only came out here because you wanted to do this, Carter. It's not my thing." This is not entirely true, but I'm annoyed and frustrated. Maybe because it's more than I can actually handle.

Besides, there's no archaeological site out here. Grant already said he didn't see anything. I might as well have stayed home.

Carter wrinkles his brow. "I didn't make you come. I don't want you to do stuff you don't want to do, Tuesday."

"But if I don't . . ." I'm not sure how to put this. "I mean, you always do stuff you don't want to do, with me. So I should do the same."

Carter gives me a puzzled look. "If I didn't want to do stuff, Tuesday, I wouldn't do it."

I swallow. "I just don't want you to find other friends who like doing this adventure-time stuff, and then you won't be my friend anymore." There. I said it. It makes me feel exposed, like I took a Band-Aid off a cut that needs to heal. My face gets hot.

Carter's expression softens. "That's not true." He comes over to me. "Tuesday, you and I are friends. We're always going to be friends."

The way he says it sounds like he's stating a true fact, as if he'd said that lemons are yellow or Earth is round. I believe him.

Grant wipes an eye. "This reminds me of my friend Trevor from childhood. We're still buddies to this day. You know, friendship isn't a finite thing, kids. It's not like you get one cup of it to spread around. There's plenty for everyone."

Carter and I can be friends even if we don't do everything together, or we both make other friends. "We're stuck together, forever." I smile. Carter fist-bumps me.

Grant has to blow his nose, and Carter groans. "Grant. You're such a softie."

Grant shrugs. "Hey, what do you want? I'm an emotional guy." He grins at me. "So do you want to give it another try, or take more of a break?"

I'm still not ready to climb up. "Can I watch for a little bit?"

"Of course."

Carter scrambles up like a monkey. He reaches the ledge at the edge of the cave. He sticks his face in there.

"Hey, there's some kind of nest up here!"

"A nest of what? Snakes?" Grant says, only half joking.

"No." Carter turns his head, his eyes wide. "I think they're owls!"

17

"Mexican spotted owls?" I squeak. I've always wanted to see one—but they live high up, in these slot canyons, where I don't go. Myra sometimes has kids' classes and she told us that usually they live in trees—but here in the canyons, they've adapted to living in the rock walls. They're not endangered, but threatened—that means eventually they could become endangered, which means they could become extinct. "I want to see."

"Come on!" Carter scoots over a couple inches, his elbows resting on the ledge.

I look uncertainly at the route up. I want to do it, but I'm afraid. Grant bends close. "If you fall, I'll spot you. Make sure you land on the mat."

I nod, taking in a deep breath. If I want to see owls, this is how I have to do it. I think of all the times Uncle Ezra tried to get me to climb with him and all the times I said no. I always thought if I waited, I'd be braver. And he always said, "Maybe next time!" in the most patient Ezra way.

I waited too long, I guess.

Suddenly I'm determined, as if Ezra were here right now asking me. I can do this. "Coming up!"

I put my feet and hands into the starting positions, then put one hand up higher, then one foot up, then repeat with the other hand and foot. It's a little bit like climbing a zigzagging ladder. Grant directs me. "To your left, Tuesday. Put your hand to the left." I see the faint white dust that Carter's left behind and put my hands in the same places.

I keep concentrating on where my hands and feet go, climbing up and up. Then I make a mistake.

I turn my head to see where Grant is, and he and the ground look very, very far away. The earth seems to spin violently, as if I'm on a merry-go-round.

"Ahhhh!" I turn my face back to the rock.

"Tuesday, you're almost here." Carter sounds very close, and he is—a couple feet above me. Now he's sitting on the ledge, motioning for me to come up.

I hoist myself upward and reach for the last rock, Carter putting a steadying hand on my shoulders. I scoot onto the ledge on my belly, then sit up next to him. It's colder here, the cave little more than a narrow indentation in the rocks that goes about ten feet back. A little light comes in from some hole far above us.

"Great job, Tuesday!" Grant calls. "Don't worry, I'll come up and help you down."

Carter grabs my arm. "Look!" He points.

I peer upward, but I hear it before I see it. Squawking. My eyes finally adjust. There's a nest of owls—two chicks and I assume the mother. The mother's got all her feathers, white spots against tan, and has huge black eyes. The chicks aren't brand-new; they're pretty big, with downy feathers, their eyeballs taking up most of their skulls.

"They," I say, "are the cutest things to ever exist."

Grant's head appears behind me, and he snaps a photo with his long-lens camera. "Wow! We're so lucky to see these. I've never seen them in here before. I'll tell Myra," he says. "You never know where an animal will pop up."

I wonder if any humans ever used this little cave for anything. I kind of doubt it, considering it would be hard to get up here while you were carrying things. I think about Ezra's poem. *Beyond the owl's pinions.* That's someplace high. Higher than where I went on the mesa.

"I have an idea." I sit extra still, because I'm excited and don't want to fall off. "I think Uncle Ezra wants me to climb."

CHAPTER

18

"Hey!"

I don't have to turn my head to recognize Carter's voice. "Good morning."

It's eleven the next day, and Carter and I are meeting at the shuttle. We're going into town to see Danielle and develop the photos I took at Hedges a few days ago so we can add them to the Instagram. We climb on board, and the shuttle lurches away.

"I've made a new checklist for figuring out Ezra's puzzle." I show Carter.

Find a higher point near the camping site

Go there, repeat search for archaeological artifacts

It's just that I don't know where there's a higher site near where we camped, or what would be up there, or why Ezra would even put that in his poem and make it extra super difficult.

Carter frowns. "So where do you think your uncle

wants you to go? How many spots are higher over there?"

"Not many. I don't remember." I frown. The other problem is, I'm sure Ezra didn't do any rock climbing the last time he was here. "I'll have you do that part."

"At your service." Carter salutes me. "Hey, do you have a copy of the poem? I want to read it again."

I take out my notebook. "Maybe you can figure out what the next step should be."

His finger traces the words. Then he looks up. "Tuesday. I don't want to be a spoilsport for the whole archaeology thing . . . but . . ."

"Tell me. I can take it." I wait.

He reads aloud:

Please find it right away
To sleep there again
For a price I never wanted to pay

"And?" I say, not understanding.

"Why does he say *to sleep there again / for a price I never wanted to pay?*" Carter asks. "What does that have to do with archaeology?"

I think and think but can't come up with a good answer. "I don't know," I admit. I look out the window at all the cars coming into the park, an endless stream as far as I can see. Carter's right.

We're back at the beginning with this whole thing. If

his poem's not about archaeology, then (a) I don't have a way to save Hedges and (b) I still don't know what my uncle means with this poem. It's double bad.

Suddenly I feel the opposite of what that botanist thought I was. Not smart at all. Only someone who thinks they're bright but actually knows absolutely nothing. "Maybe we should just go home. I don't even feel like developing the photos anymore." I can barely get up the energy to push the words out of my mouth.

"It's okay, Tuesday," Carter reassures me. "We'll figure it out."

"But if there's no new site, then Hedges is doomed."

Carter doesn't have anything to say to that.

The shuttle stops at the last stop, the visitor center. We climb off and start walking out of the park to get to the bus stop. The sun's especially hot today, and I wish I'd brought a hat as we stand there waiting.

To sleep there again
For a price I never wanted to pay

I lean against the bus stop sign, thinking about turning around and going back to bed. "Is this all a waste of time? Who cares if we have photos of Hedges on Instagram?"

"I mean, I do." Carter pushes a pebble around with his shoe. He sounds disappointed. It wouldn't be fair to him if I skipped out on Danielle. "I think people want to see Hedges the way it is now. In case it's all destroyed later."

Carter's right. "Okay." I shake myself out of my sour mood a little. "I did want to show you how cool it is to develop the prints, though. Danielle knows a lot."

My throat clenches as I remember something. What Danielle said about how her late husband told her where to put his ashes. *Roses are red, violets are blue, put my ashes on Mount Rainier or I'll always haunt you.*

My heart skids to a stop, practically. "What if . . . ?"

"What if what?" Carter squints at me.

"What if Uncle Ezra is actually telling me where to put his ashes?" I ask slowly.

Carter hops up and down like a bunny. "Oh my gosh! I bet you're right. I mean, it makes more sense. When my dad died, he told us to put his ashes in this man-made coral reef thing. People say that kind of thing right before they pass away."

My hands have suddenly gone cold, and I put them under my armpits. "Yeah. That does make more sense." But I'm still stuck on the whole "no archaeology" part. And even if I've figured out the right question for the poem, "Where should we put Uncle Ezra's ashes?" I've still got no answer.

My eyes fill, and I drop my chin so my hair blocks them.

"Aren't you happy that you figured out what the puzzle is for, at least?" Carter asks.

I nod slowly. "I am. I am. But it means that Hedges is gone, for real."

Carter sighs. "Yeah, Tuesday. I guess maybe it does."

On the bus, we pass by Hedges, where the construction crew is hard at work. Tractors and earth movers send up great clouds of brown-red dust. "This is so depressing," Carter says. "It's going to be just like any other place in the world."

I don't respond, because there's nothing else I can say. I don't even feel like developing the photos now. I feel like I've failed Uncle Ezra in a big way. If his poem's not about archaeology but about the place he wants us to put his ashes, I'm still no closer to figuring out where that is. I want to lie on the couch and eat potato chips and chocolate. But Carter wants to see how the photos get developed, so I'll do it for him. I look at my watch. "We're like forty minutes early for Danielle."

Carter pulls out a twenty-dollar bill. "Come on. My mom said to treat you. Let's go to the coffee shop."

I sit outside at a little wrought iron table to hold it while Carter goes inside. Even though it's hot, Ezra always told me that I should get about twenty minutes of sun a day, for vitamin D's sake. "Not too much or you'll get burned," he said. "But most people are vitamin D-deficient." This makes me think again about how unfair his death was, that he did everything right and still passed away.

I sigh, then take out my notebook and the list I just made. I cross it all out.

Uncle Ezra wouldn't want me to give up. Now that I'm not looking for an archaeological site, is there any other way I can stop construction? I think and think. Tourists come in and out with their coffees—there must be a long line. I write a new title, *How to Stop Them From Developing Hedges Ranch, Without Archaeology*, but that doesn't help. My mind's blank.

Carter finally comes out with two iced chocolate drinks and two croissants on plates, somehow balancing them all effortlessly. "Here you go."

"Thanks." I take the treat and bite into it. The buttery, flaky layers make me forget my troubles for a minute. "Do you think they're happier in France?"

"Why?"

"Because they eat these for breakfast every day."

"Do they?" Carter shrugs. "Probably, then."

I turn the paper around to show him. "Any ideas?"

"Get a bunch of people to protest?" Carter suggests. I write this down.

"Get someone else to buy it?" I say. "But this company already bought it, so I don't think they'll sell it."

"I mean, I think the bouldering school people would

protest, too," Carter says.

"Are they even going to care, as long as they can still go bouldering?" I ask.

"Lots of them are conservationists. They don't want to deal with extra traffic and stuff, either."

I write that down. *Bouldering school.* "We could also email the local schools. Maybe a petition?"

"Yeah," Carter says. I write that down.

"What else?" I ask. Neither of these things seem like they'd lead to any direct results. There aren't enough people locally to protest, to make a huge difference to the developers.

"Let the air out of the tractor tires?" Carter grins to let me know he's joking. "Replace all the construction workers with secret environmentalists working for us?"

"Now you're being silly." But he does have a point. The only things we can think of are unreasonable.

Once, Uncle Ezra was helping me with a math problem I couldn't figure out. "This is impossible," I told him. I was so frustrated I was actually crying—and it takes a lot to make me feel that helpless. "There is no answer."

"There is an answer, Tuesday," Ezra said. "In science, we don't know the answer until we've exhausted all the paths. But we don't know ahead of time what path to pick, or even what possible paths might exist. You have to explore. Take a break. Keep trying later."

So I took a break. I took a nap and had a snack and

read a book. Finally, later, I came back and tried the math problem a totally different way, a way that didn't work. But that way made me think of another approach. And finally, it worked.

I write, *Find a new path.*

A little later, Danielle lets us in, and I introduce her to Carter. "Do you like photography, too?" she asks.

Carter nods. "I mean, not like Tuesday does."

"He took the photo of the valley. It was his idea to put the boulder in the foreground."

"Impressive!"

Carter blushes. He's not used to being artistic, either.

Danielle checks behind us. "Where's Silas?"

"I don't know." I hesitate. "Am I not supposed to come without him?"

"No, it's fine." She shrugs. "He hasn't answered my texts—but then again he doesn't have great cell service. I wanted to see if he'd like to do a lecture at the rec center before he leaves."

"Interesting." I know he drives to different places, like the administration building parking lot, to receive his messages, so he should have responded. But he didn't.

"He's probably busy hiking or doing art stuff." Carter looks at Danielle's photos. "These are really cool."

"You can go ahead into the darkroom if you remember everything," Danielle says. "I trust you, and everything is poured out into the trays already. Just don't mix chemicals together."

I frown. I'm not sure I can remember all the steps without Silas here. I've only done it once. "Can you help me?"

Danielle smiles. "Happy to."

We go in the darkroom. "Whoa! This is like a Halloween haunted house with this red light." Carter turns in a circle.

"Your eyes will get used to it in a minute," Danielle says.

She's got some prints drying on the line. These are of the night sky, stars twinkling dimly. "Do you take a lot of night photos?" I ask.

"I used to." She smiles at me. "When my husband was alive. Now my knees bother me too much. Getting old isn't for the weak."

"What does that mean? You'll get old whether or not you're weak." I think of Ezra. "Isn't it better than being dead?"

Carter chimes in. "My grandparents say it literally every time I see them."

My grandparents died when I was little, a few years apart from each other. Dana used a donor for my father, so I don't know who my father's parents are and I probably never will. Which is fine with me. I'd rather be here through a donor than not at all.

Carter's grandparents live near Las Vegas. He sees them every couple of months and talks to them on the phone all the time. Sometimes I'm jealous of that. Because if he has to complain about his parents or wants a break, he can talk to his grandparents, like I did with Uncle Ezra.

Once in a while, I'd be having some problem that Dana didn't fully understand, so I'd talk to Ezra. Like I said, Ezra was more like me than my mother, so he always got me in ways Dana can't. I don't have any other adults besides Dana in my family now.

"Well." Danielle pauses to consider. In the red light the wrinkles on her face are smoothed out. "I suppose because when you hit forty, your body starts falling apart. You start getting various aches and pains, and then you're hobbling toward old age. That's why this is a saying."

She's the only adult who ever explained it to me. "Thanks."

"Don't mention it." She reaches over and ruffles my hair, which feels like the strands are pulling out of my head. I cringe, pulling back. "I'm sorry, did that hurt?"

"Yes," I say, though she didn't yank on my hair and it's hard for me to explain exactly how it feels.

"She doesn't like to be touched, generally." Carter pulls out a stack of photos and looks through them.

I confirm. "Correct. It's not my thing." That's one

thing I remember my grandparents doing—I didn't like to hug and they got mad at Dana for it. But Dana told them I didn't have to let anyone touch me, grandparent or not.

"That's fine," Danielle says. "All of us have different preferences. You remind me of my own granddaughter, who doesn't mind. But I should never presume."

I smile, instantly forgiving her. "No worries." It's always surprising, somehow, when adults admit to making errors. I like it. I wish Dana would do it more.

We make the negatives and then the prints, and then go back into the main room. Danielle shows me and Carter her digital camera as the prints dry. I love looking at all the controls. "So many settings."

"Not too many more than a regular camera. Sure, it's got this landscape-mode feature and a night feature, but I always set it myself to get it right." She nods at Carter. "Want to go get the proofs?"

Carter disappears into the darkroom, then returns. He's squinting at one of the proofs. "What is this thing?"

I go over and look. In one of the photos from Hedges by the hoodoo and the tree, there's an animal in the foreground. "Is that a gopher?"

"Let me see." Danielle comes over and puts her reading glasses on. "Some kind of animal, all right. Happens to me all the time. Animals popping up out of nowhere trying to get their moment of fame." She puts the photo on the table and uses the photographer's loupe. "Huh."

"What?" Carter and I both say.

"Looks like a prairie dog to me. They have them in Oklahoma, where I'm from. Never seen one here." She squints at the picture. "Some people keep them as pets, even."

Interesting. I've never seen one in the time we've been living at the park. I think I would have seen one or heard about it, if they were common, the way you know there are rabbits and foxes and deer—because they're around. "I don't think that's it. Hedges isn't really a prairie."

"It has meadows and things like a prairie, though," Danielle says. "Let's blow this up."

Using the negative to get the details, we make another print. "We're going to ignore the rest of this photo for now and focus on the animal," Danielle says. I hold a piece of cardboard over the dark area, and she turns on the light.

Then we look at the photo. Now I can see that it's standing on its hind legs, but the details aren't super clear. "It still looks like a gopher to me."

"Prairie dogs are about as big as a rabbit. Gophers are smaller. Was it that big?"

I shake my head. "I didn't see it at all in real life. The camera captured it." It's hard to tell the scale on the photo. It's not like there's a ruler next to the animal's head or something. I squint, but there's no way I can tell what it is. It might have a tail behind it that I can't see and be a regular squirrel. "Let's take it to Myra."

"Good idea," Carter says.

Danielle helps us make eight-by-ten prints of the others, but I can't stop thinking about the prairie dog. If there are no prairie dogs in Utah, then would they be considered an endangered animal here? And then the construction people would have to stop.

We use our phones to take pictures of the prints, then we upload the photos one by one to Instagram. I write the captions. Carter adds a bunch of hashtags, including #conservation and #nature and #LylaRedding. "Why Lyla? She's not in the picture. Why would she care?" I ask.

"Because there are a million people following her. That means more eyeballs on your photos."

I still don't get why so many people follow her. Her stuff's not very useful for the most part. But then, I guess it's probably not meant for me. "Hmph."

"You sound like me," Danielle says. "I detest social media."

"I'm not against social media. Only useless social media." I think about Dana's worries—what if some weirdo who follows Lyla Redding starts messaging us? I'd tell Dana and block, but it seems like a hassle. Then again, someone who's bothering a kid should be punished, not me. It's not my responsibility.

Carter shrugs. "Just saying. It could help."

"All right, let's do an experiment," I tell him. "Tag some pictures with her name and don't tag others. Then we'll see which ones do better."

"Deal," he says. I take out the Hedges checklist and add:

> *Find out if there are rare prairie dogs here. Will this stop construction?*
> *Tag some photos with Lyla's name; compare with the others. See what happens.*

Carter tags the animal photo with Lyla Redding and not the others. "Now let's see what happens. What's your hypothesis, Doctor?"

I take on a British accent. "Well, Doctor, I do believe that these will perform the same."

"Respectfully disagree, Doctor."

"Agree to disagree, Doctor."

We shake hands. For the first time in a while, I feel like I'm having fun again. This is the kind of thing Carter and I do. And that Ezra and I did. We would pretend to be ridiculous gold miners together. At the thought, a pang hits my chest and I pause.

It's funny how almost anything can make me think of Ezra.

Danielle, watching us, snorts with laughter. "You two

are the most entertaining thing to happen around here for a long time. Let's get you a snack."

We both salute her. "Sounds good to me," I say. Ezra would want me to have a good time. He'd tell me to move on. He'd tell Dana the same. But how can we when we don't even know who we are without him?

CHAPTER

19

While we're still at Danielle's, Carter emails the bouldering school to ask if they want to try to stop the Hedges development. Then we take the bus back to the park, stopping at the administrative offices. "Hey, kids," Shawn the bat guy greets us in the science bungalow. His space is by the entrance, so he's sort of the unofficial greeter. That's what everyone calls him—Bat Guy. Part of his office has been made into a closet so he can hang up all his roping equipment. All he does is climb and track bats.

"Hey!" Of course Carter likes talking to Shawn, since they both love climbing. He stops and they start chattering about rocks.

I continue down the hall. Dana's little whiteboard says *In the Field* and her door is locked, but Myra's door is open and she's at her computer. "Myra, can I show you something?"

"Hey, Tuesday! Sure." She turns from her computer, taking off her glasses. She blinks. Her brown eyeliner's a little smeared. "I could use a break."

I show her the photo. "Look at this and tell me what kind of animal it is. It's in Hedges."

"Hmmm." She frowns, puts her glasses back on. "What did its tail look like? A gopher has a hairless tail."

"I don't know, I didn't see it in person." I explain how I got the photo.

"Could be a ground squirrel or a gopher." She purses her lips. "Probably a gopher. Was it by itself?"

I shrug. Did she not hear what I said? I'm not the only one with selective listening. "Like I said, this is the only one I saw."

"We have pocket gophers around here. They're small. Smaller than squirrels. This was bigger than a squirrel, fatter, too."

"I don't think it's as small as a pocket gopher. I've seen those." But as I speak, I'm not sure. I wish there was at least a rock next to it for size purposes. "Danielle, the photographer lady, says it looks like a prairie dog from Oklahoma."

Carter comes in as Myra leans back in her chair. "Those live in the plains, like in Oklahoma. But they did reintroduce them to Arches National Park a few years ago."

Arches is another park in Utah. It's not that close, but

not horribly far either. I think of Hedges and the farm-land that the Mormons made. "But there are plains inside Hedges. Even if they're mostly man-made." Besides, the place where I took the photo was like a plain. It was flat. Maybe she would call that a meadow, though.

Myra takes off her glasses and wipes under her eyes. "It's improbable, Tuesday."

"Is it impossible, though?" I prod her.

Myra gives me a long stare that reminds me of Dana. "No. Not impossible."

"Why isn't it?" Carter asks, and I want to shush him. Myra is getting more annoyed by the second.

Myra crosses her arms. "I suppose they could have made their way down from the Arches area in a few years. Or maybe they were always at Hedges and we never saw them because nobody's been back where you took the photos for decades."

"Are they endangered?" I ask.

"Prairie dogs? No. I mean, they live all over the US. They're basically like ground squirrels." She puts her hand back on her mouse, getting ready to work. "Not special at all."

"Even if none of them live here?" I ask.

"That's not really how it works," Myra says.

So even if there were prairie dogs there, it wouldn't help anything. Every muscle in my body seems to melt in disappointment. "Thanks, Myra."

"No problem." She shrugs. "Maybe it's the angle of the photo making a pocket gopher look big. Cameras are funny."

"Maybe." I don't think this is the case, but it's another time when arguing is pointless.

We leave the science offices and walk slowly across the parking lot toward the road. The sun seems to press down on me, crushing my lungs. Or maybe that's what defeat feels like.

I'm not sure what else I can do. If Myra doesn't believe it's a prairie dog, there's no way I can go back into Hedges to look for them. Much less any archaeological sites, since I'm not even allowed to hike back there alone again. "I guess Hedges is a thing that's going to happen."

I kick a stone out of my way. I think about Uncle Ezra, and how horrified he'd be if he saw what was happening. He'd probably do something like chain himself to one of the grapevines. Dana would never.

Carter stops moving. "Wait. Can you show me where you took the photo? Maybe we can find the prairie dog ourselves."

"What does it matter?"

"Because even if they got here via Arches, it would be interesting to know. I bet the biologists who work on those would want to find that out," Carter says.

This is true. And if Carter comes with me, I won't be alone. "I think that's an excellent idea."

We've just come out from the underpass when we see Silas's car parked on the side of the road. He sits in a folding camp chair, an easel set up in front of him, painting, a palette in his right hand and a paintbrush in his left. He's wearing a volunteer ranger outfit—khaki button-up short sleeve shirt and brown pants, with a big hat. It's not odd, because all the artists have to be volunteer park rangers, which means they go around and talk to people about the program, or they sit and do their artwork and people come talk to them, Dana says.

"Hey! Aren't you supposed to be volunteering?"

"I got tired of hikers interrupting me to ask where the bathrooms are." Silas purses his lips. "What kind of trouble are you two getting into?"

We look at each other and shrug.

"Uh-oh." He stretches out his long legs. "Tell me."

I take out the photo and show him. "What do you think that is?"

"It's a prairie dog." He hands it back. "I had one as a pet growing up."

"See?" Carter says. "It could be significant."

I'm about to explain everything to Silas and step around closer to him, but then I catch sight of his canvas. He's painting the underpass and the road above it. The thick black line of the asphalt cuts through the natural beauty.

"Why not? It's part of the land now." He dips his brush into some bright-yellow paint and dabs at the canvas. "Sorry, kids. Can't talk. I have to work fast. I'm using acrylics, and they dry out."

I stand watching him paint, wondering how long it took him to figure out how to do this. "Were you always good at art?"

"I was always interested. But not super good, no. I worked at it." He continues to dab the canvas. I examine his face from the side. His eyes are still puffy, but more like . . . blank. Not sad. Not happy. Not anything at all. His face is a blank mask, kind of like Lyla Redding's was.

"Are you okay?" I ask him.

Silas doesn't answer. He bats away a fly buzzing at his face.

Carter tugs at my arm. "Let's let him do his thing, Tuesday."

I resist him. "One more thing. Danielle says you haven't responded to her. Have you gotten her messages?"

"Yup. I did. I will." Silas mutters something to himself and swats away another insect. "These horseflies bite!"

"You should wear repellent," I tell him, and then Carter drags me away. I wait until we're out of Silas's hearing before I speak. "There's something wrong with him."

"Grant says there's something wrong with all artists," Carter says, then chuckles as if that's funny.

"Not like that."

"He does seem a little down. But hey"—Carter shrugs—"We can't fix everything, can we?"

"I don't even know if we can fix one thing."

"At least he told us it was a prairie dog. That's one more vote for."

I suppose that's true. I look back at Silas, and he's stopped painting, leaning forward, his arms on his knees and his head down.

20

D ana drives me to the east entrance side of the park for dinner. We don't go there often. You have to drive up a winding road called the 9. If you're not used to it, it can make you feel nauseous. When you look down all you see is cliff. You look up and see cars above you, and that's a little odd, too.

I'm glad to have this time with her. Maybe she's coming out of her weird fog where it didn't seem like she cared about anything. I decide to tell Dana about the animal that might be a prairie dog while we eat our dinner. I'll show her the photo and see what she says.

Tourists drive slow. Dana drives like there's someone chasing her, at the top of the speed limit, used to making these turns and not having her car fly off the side of the cliff. If archaeology doesn't work out, she could probably be a race car driver.

There are two tunnels built into the mountains.

The first one is over a mile long, and it's bumpy and dark. There are a few windows cut into the tunnel— sometimes tourists try to stop there even though signs say no stopping.

Today, the ranger stops the FedEx driver and uses her radio to shut the tunnel from the other side. The delivery truck is so tall it has to go in the middle of the tunnel to fit, which means it drives in both lanes.

So we drive on through, following FedEx.

The east side is higher in elevation. Closer to the sky. Better for stars.

We drive through all the mountains, past this hill called Checkerboard Mesa—because the stone colors make it look like a giant's checkerboard—to a restaurant on the other side.

When we open the door, the bell jingles, and it feels like walking into a full-size refrigerator. Goose bumps rise on my skin, in a good way. The server tells us to sit anywhere, so I choose a booth by the window and slide across the cracked brown vinyl. We used to come here with Ezra but haven't been since the last summer, the last time he was here. This is a diner that could be anyplace in America, Ezra told me. "Someday we'll do a road trip and stop at all of them," he said. "Or at least a dozen."

We order burgers and cherry pie. They have good pie here.

Ezra always got the chocolate pie—he wasn't a big fan of cooked fruit.

I'm happy because it was Dana's idea to come here. It's usually me who has to suggest it, ask her to take me here and to look at stars. We haven't been to this place in months.

Being the one who thinks of things to do is all right, but it's also nice when other people do it. It's sort of like with me and Carter. We both think of things to do and invite the other person. If Carter never did, then I would think he didn't like me.

Anyway, after I'd asked to come here twice and been told no, I stopped asking.

Now it's time for me to tell Dana what I've discovered. "Guess what was in one of my photos?" I explain the whole story and show her the picture. "What if it is a prairie dog?"

She frowns at the phone. "Prairie dogs aren't very interesting. They're like squirrels."

"Yes, but it's significant that it would be in Hedges."

She shrugs. "You should listen to Myra."

I go cold. "But . . ."

"You're not the expert, Tuesday. Myra has studied this for years."

"That's true," I say. "However, she says it's not impossible."

My mother shrugs again.

It feels as if she's slammed a door in my face. I go quiet.

Obviously I respect Myra's opinion. But Myra wasn't in Hedges. I was.

It's like Uncle Ezra told us. Amateurs make discoveries all the time in astronomy. This doesn't mean that the astronomers with PhDs don't know anything. They weren't looking at the same part of the sky at that moment. And the professional astronomers respect the amateurs—they don't dismiss them.

This is like that. I'm an amateur, and I'm looking at a part of the ground that Myra hasn't.

Why can't my mother see that?

After our burgers, our cherry pies come warm and with a scoop of the locally made vanilla ice cream, plus whipped cream. Dana has coffee with hers. I have a glass of milk.

"Cheers," Dana says, and holds up her coffee cup. I clink my milk glass against it.

"Cheers," I say.

I'm five bites in when I look across the table and realize my mother's not eating. Her hands are cupped around the mug.

"Are you full?" I ask. Though she barely touched her burger.

Dana shakes her head. "I wanted to talk to you about something."

Oh. I rest my fork across the pie plate. My stomach clenches, and a dozen possibilities fly through my head. Is the park closing? Is she going to jail? "What is it?" I ask, impatient, because she hasn't said anything.

"I applied for a job at South Dakota State," Dana says. "Tenure track. I have a video interview tomorrow."

What? The ice cream's melting into a puddle, and my stomach turns. I push the plate away. "You complained about how crowded the park's getting, but you never said you were actually applying to jobs." I don't meet her eyes. Why would she do that and not tell me? What else is she not telling me about? A hot bolt of anger rises.

"I didn't want to say anything unless it came to fruition. But yeah, I've been looking for a while."

She should have told me, because I would have said no, and then everyone wouldn't have wasted their time. "I don't want to move."

Dana sighs. "You know the park's been difficult to deal with lately—the lack of funding, the overcrowding."

I nod. I pick up the napkin and twist it tightly into a coil. "It's been that way forever."

"I'm burned out. That's the truth." Dana reaches over the table for me. I draw my hands into my lap so she can't reach them. "I love my job, but I love you more. I have to take care of myself so I can take care of you. And this university will be in a real town, where you can go to a regular school."

"I don't want to." I bite my lip. "I don't want to leave Carter."

"And this whole thing with Hedges—it's the cherry on top. No pun intended." She points at my pie. "You should eat that."

"You should eat yours. Keep your eye on your own plate." I mean to sound joking, but I sound super harsh. That ranch development is ruining everything.

"I should." Dana takes a tiny bite of pie.

I pull my plate toward me and start in again. The pie's a little bit tart, which is good with the sweet creaminess of the ice cream. I concentrate on that for a few seconds, which makes me feel calmer. But then thoughts crowd my mind. How can I leave Carter behind? He'll be the only kid in our age range in the park. I don't want to go to South Dakota. Zion can get cold, but snow usually doesn't stick for long. South Dakota is a whole other story.

"If you were going to apply someplace new, why couldn't you apply to the University of Hawaii?" I drink some milk.

"If you want to teach at a university, you have to apply at the places that have jobs open."

"Why do you want to be in a university instead of out in the field? I think you'll be unhappy."

She shakes her head. "I don't want you to worry about

my happiness, Tuesday." Her face closes off as she slips into parent mode. "Now finish your pie. It's almost dark enough for stars."

"I don't have my telescope."

"I brought it." She smiles big. But I'm mad because I thought she was inviting me to get dinner to be nice, and obviously she only did it to bribe me or something.

I don't finish my pie. She can't tell me not to worry about her happiness—why shouldn't I be worried about it? She's my mother. I imagine Ezra here, telling her not to lose what she has in Zion. He was always jealous of her job, saying he was stuck at the university. "What do you think Ezra would have said about it?"

She blinks at me like an owl, slowly, with wide eyes. "Why do you ask?"

I shrug. "I just wondered."

"It doesn't matter," she says, her voice tense. "Ezra had his own opinions, and I have mine."

I lean back. "So you know he would've told you it was a bad idea."

She throws some bills on the table, then stands. "Listen. Ezra's gone, and we don't know what he would've said. And it's my life, and yours. Not his."

I stare at my mother, trying to get through. Then I remember what Carter suggested earlier. Maybe that will affect Dana. "He wanted us to spread his ashes here," I say suddenly. "That's what the poem's about. And isn't that a more reasonable explanation than archaeology?"

She closes her eyes for a moment. "I can't . . . I can't talk about this right now. I have to pee." She says that last part so loud that a few customers look up. Embarrassing. She heads toward the restrooms.

I swallow. Why doesn't she care about what I think anymore? I don't want to leave. I want to stay here forever. Hanging out with Carter. Going out with the wildlife biologist to look at animals and my mother to look at ruins and learn history. I know how lucky I am.

But she doesn't want to talk, so there's nothing I can do.

I text Carter. I start out by typing exactly what happened. *Dana's interviewing for a job in another state.* I stare at the text. Typing it and seeing it written in words sends a cold shudder through me. This is real. I don't send it.

My phone startles me by buzzing in my hand. It's Carter. He's sent me an image of what the bouldering school said.

Because our school will remain open, and because a good portion of the space will still be preserved, we don't think it's necessary to do anything at this time.

At this time? If not now, when? I delete the text I wrote. *Disappointing,* I respond. Then I cross *that* off the list.

Do you want to go to the ranch tomorrow and look for that prairie dog/gopher? Carter texts.

YES.

No need to shout

I smile. I don't know what I would do without Carter. How can I move to South Dakota and start all over again?

I don't have my notebook with me, so I type a note into my phone to add to my checklist:

Prove the existence of the prairie dog in Hedges.

But even if there are a billion prairie dogs there (an exaggeration, you'd definitely see them then), will it make a bit of difference to the development? I'm not sure. Anyway, the prairie dog question is something that needs to be answered. It would be weird if they were in Hedges. It's got to mean something else.

I just don't know what it is.

I have to follow this new path. It's the only one we have right now. Maybe we'll think of something else while we're at Hedges tomorrow.

By the time Dana gets back, I'm waiting by the door. She smiles at me like everything is fine, and this makes me angry all over again. I want to tell her to stop pretending, but I have the feeling it's going to tip over into a big thing again.

I push it open for her, and she walks out into the balmy night, the hot air feeling like a relief after how cold it was inside. The stars twinkle in the sky, appearing close enough to touch. "Want to go to our usual spot?" That's the fourth turnoff after the second tunnel. We park and set up the telescope right by the car.

"No." I get in the car. "I want to go home."

CHAPTER

21

Whenever Dana and I have a disagreement and it gets emotional, we have a pattern. First we give each other time to calm down. Then Dana knocks on my door and we have a calm, rational discussion in which we solve the problem. Like when we had a disagreement about the amount of screen time I get—she wanted me to have zero more, I wanted an hour. I negotiated for fifteen more minutes.

This time, though, she does not knock on my door. I don't go in there. I can't shake the sense that she's betraying me. So instead, I fall asleep with a book in my face. In the morning, I wake when her car starts in the driveway.

I go eat my breakfast. Dana's left a sticky note on the box, with a heart. "Have a great day." At least I know she's not mad at me. I'm not mad at her, either. Just . . . puzzled. I don't understand why she's practicing avoidance, something she tells me I shouldn't do.

I get all my photography equipment together; then I go to Carter's. He's someone who gets up with the sun and spends the morning doing a bunch of things. Sometimes he and his mom go running. Other times he does his chores.

He's waiting for me when I get there, looking more alert than I feel. He waves a bag of peanut M&M's in my general direction. "Look what I have!"

I grin. My favorite.

We eat them on the way to the shuttle, not talking, crunching the peanuts. I think about telling him what Dana said last night, and a few times I try, but then stop and ask myself why. It will ruin this morning.

Besides, she might not even get the job. So there's no point in worrying about it yet.

"And guess what's happening on Instagram." Carter pulls out his phone. "The animal photo we tagged with Lyla Redding got over a hundred likes, and the other ones only got like fifteen." He sounds a little smug. "Plus we have more than five hundred followers now."

I wish Carter hadn't been right about this, because it means that people care more about Lyla than they do about actual conservation. "Maybe it's because there's a cute animal in that one. We can't account for the cuteness factor in a science experiment, can we?" I slap my hand on my forehead. "Ugh. We should have compared two animal photos instead!"

"That might have had something to do with it. But maybe not. We don't know for sure." He shows me his phone. "Check out these comments."

Squirrel!

Not a squirrel, that's a common guinea pig, we have them here

Looks like a prairie dog to me

Def prairie dog

Are we sure that's not a large rat

Ugh. Gophers. Get them all the time here. They ate my carrots! And I worked hard on those carrots!

"These are kind of useless comments." I hand Carter his phone.

He shrugs. "That's like ninety-nine percent of the internet."

I laugh.

"I was thinking"—Carter holds up his phone—"if we're going to use the Instagram account to help with Hedges, we should change the name to something like StopHedgesRanch."

I consider this. "But people wouldn't search by the name Hedges, because nobody really knows about it."

"True. So something with Zion in it."

I think about what my goal is. To stop Hedges from getting developed because I want to keep the skies dark and the land clear. "Keep Zion Dark?"

Carter's face lights up. "By Jove, I've think we've got it," he says in his fake British accent. He grabs my backpack and takes out my notebook. The checklist page is marked with a bright-orange sticky tab. He writes:

Change Instagram name
Get new followers so people know about Hedges
Tell people about the prairie dog
Ask people to take action

"How do we get more followers?" I ask. "Pay?"

"No. That's useless, and Instagram doesn't like it." Carter makes another note: *Leave comments on other Instagram accounts so people will come over and look at ours and hopefully follow us.*

"That sounds time-consuming," I say. "And you're being too wordy for a checklist."

"I use as many words as I need," Carter says. "I'll do the commenting on the other accounts, okay? I've got the internet."

"Sounds good to me," I say.

The streets of Springdale crawl with tourists. Sometimes there are so many standing on the sidewalks that Carter and I have to walk single file on the way to the ranch.

I've never walked into Hedges on foot. We pass under the gate that says *Hedges* in burnt-out letters on wood. The front part used to be all vineyard. There's a construction crew, and the vineyard is fenced off with orange plastic netting. The ground's all smoothed out now, the vines dug up, and a cement truck pours concrete.

"Wow," Carter says. "They moved fast."

I shrug. "Those vines were mostly dead anyway." I'm repeating what Dana said, as if I don't care, but I do. It makes my stomach hurt.

We walk by some construction workers, but nobody says anything. I wonder if we're allowed to be in here, but people are coming in for bouldering lessons, so I don't think they'll mind.

However. The part I want to go to is the part where only Dana and her crew are allowed.

But I'm part of Dana's crew, I argue with myself. I can do it. And this is of the utmost importance.

We walk in along the side of the road, passing by the rock-climbing place, where there's some kids climbing. "Hey, Carter!" somebody shouts.

"Hey!" Carter waves. "See you tomorrow."

"Oh." I get a little bit of a queasy jealous feeling. Not because I don't want Carter to have more friends— more because *I* don't have more friends. Sometimes Carter's busy, and it'd be nice if I had more people to hang out with. But it's not like I can order friends on the internet. I have to deal with being by myself a lot. Which is easier said than done.

What will it be like in South Dakota? Will I be able to make new friends there? I'm not sure.

We keep walking past the place where Dana's crew works sometimes. Nobody's here today. I lead Carter back into the canyon, to the fork. "How far did you go?" he asks.

"I guess it is kind of far." I hadn't realized quite how long it took.

The meadow's like I remember it. "I used string to mark where I looked. Do you see it?" I scan the ground. All I see are branches and grass and things like that.

"This string?" Carter points to a tangle of white.

I groan. The string got blown away. "I didn't stick the branches down into the ground far enough."

"But was it near here?"

I squint at the ground. "Generally?" It's so hard to tell. I think I see the tree branch I took a photo of—except, no, that's not the same one. I bring up the photo on my phone. If it is, more branches got blown down around it. I guess the branch I chose wasn't unique enough to be a landmark. I blow air out of my nose, frustrated with myself. "I should've been more careful."

"You know what Grant says about hindsight." Carter points at his eyes.

"Twenty-twenty," we say at the same time.

Carter points at the sandy ground, at some faint little footprints. It looks like a breeze could blow them away at any second. "Look at that."

"Raccoon?" Carter and I both learned about footprints as soon as we got here. It's like a city kid knowing about the traffic light system. It's something you learn. That and animal poop. We both had copies of a book called *Who Pooped in the Park?* that describes animal poops. Most are easy—deer poop looks like pebbles, sometimes with berry things mixed in. Mountain lion poop is huge. Sheep droppings can look a lot like deer's. That way, if you're hiking and you see a fresh mountain lion poop, you know you need to be careful.

"Too small."

I squat down to get a closer look. He's right. And the paws are long and thinnish, bigger than a rat's. The back paws and the front paws are different. I see three fingers on some and five on others. "I don't know. Possum?"

"Maybe. Maybe not."

"Maybe a baby."

"It would be riding on its mom," Carter points out. Possums cling to their mothers like crazy. He starts following the tracks, and I, of course, follow Carter.

We continue on and on, around some boulders and small hills and sandstone areas. I stop a few times and take photos of interesting rock formations on the earth and a piñon tree that's growing parallel to the ground, blown that way by the wind, and an interesting fallen tree. Carter loses the tracks a couple times but then finds them again.

Then Carter stops short. "Look at this." He points with his hiking boot.

It's scat—aka poop. This dropping is thin, only about an inch and a half long, with a pointy twist at the end like some animal ate a bread tie. I squat for a closer look. Pieces of fur and bone are intertwined with it. "It's a carnivore. But it's too small to be a coyote."

"Maybe the coyote has digestive issues."

I don't know if he's joking. "Possible."

He takes a photo with his phone, then checks it. "No service here. I'll look it up later."

"Wait." I carefully put my boot beside it, remembering the other animal photo. "For scale."

"Good thinking." He takes another shot.

I glance back and realize we've walked quite a way. "How far are we going to go?"

"We can head back. If we keep going, we'll meet up with where we went rock climbing the other day. I think. Remember, Grant said that canyon met up with this one?"

That's true. And that also could be how the prairie dogs made their way here. Maybe. That's something I'm not sure about.

Finally we're standing on the edge of a mesa. Below I

can see the construction crew and the valley.

"Whoa. Look at this view." Carter shades his eyes and turns to admire it all. "This is definitely where they're going to put the fancy houses."

"No way." My stomach clenches. "How are they going to get any equipment up here?"

Carter motions to me, then points down, toward the incline between us and the valley below. "This hill. They'll make a road."

I take in a breath. "I'm going to get a photo." Because this view won't be here next year. I set up the camera and put myself under the hood.

I stare into the upside-down landscape, at the rolling hills and sandstone canyon, and a sense of hollowness comes over me. Soon this place will be gone forever. I don't even want to cry. I feel inside out.

I get the picture, then stand up and start breaking down the camera. Carter looks at my face, and I know from his expression he's feeling something similar. Without having to say a word, we turn around and leave.

The way back seems much longer than the way there. It takes me a few extra minutes to pick my way down the ridge—my feet feel heavy and slippery, though they're no different than they were before I saw all that equipment.

We've come out from the fork and are heading back by the dig site when someone yells, "What are you kids doing back here?" A man in a hard hat marches toward us.

"What are *you* doing back here?" Carter stands, puts his hands on his hips. "I think we're as authorized as you. This is a sensitive area." He points at the dig site.

"Get out of here." The man makes a shooing motion with his hands as if we're some stray cats. "Go on. Get."

"We're getting." Carter shakes his head.

I hurry by the man. I try not to look at his face too closely, but I can see it's red and angry-looking. "We didn't do anything," I tell him. "It's still pristine."

"I don't care about that," he says. "We're about to take heavy equipment back there and you'd get hurt."

I stop. "Wait. Heavy equipment way back in the canyon?"

He nods.

"But what about the archaeological sites?" They're supposed to leave those alone. Those are in between the canyon and the field.

"We're going around those," the man says. "We got our clearances."

Of course. Somehow I thought the sites that Dana is working on would act as some kind of blockade, I guess. But they're going to make a wide detour around them and go back to where we were. Or as close as they can get. I kind of doubt they can get most of that equipment through.

What if they blast the walls?

"I don't want you to do that," I say to the man.

He blinks at me. "Okay. Thanks for letting me know. I really don't care."

I blush and can't tell if I'm about to cry or yell. I don't know why I said that out loud, except that I was thinking it. Carter takes my arm. "Come on."

Numbly I follow him. Sure enough, I see the archaeological sites still have their orange fencing around them, and outside of those now, tractors and bulldozers are parked, waiting. The crew's sitting around eating lunch. I wonder how they feel about destroying this place. Are they locals? Do they like to use the park?

I break off our path and go over to them. "Excuse me," I say to the first person I see, a woman with curly reddish hair eating a peanut-butter-and-jelly sandwich. "Do you know you're destroying pristine land?"

She blinks, looking amused the way adults often look at me when I say stuff like this. "Pristine?"

"Untouched. All natural."

She takes a bite of her sandwich and talks around it. "Yeah, it's pretty. It'll make nice houses."

"But don't you care?"

She shrugs. "Progress is progress, people need places to live, and I need a paycheck."

I wouldn't be able to stop caring to do something like this. I don't know if anything I say could change her mind.

"Come on, Tuesday," Carter says, and I run to catch up.

We walk past the boulders, past the construction zone, and out of the ranch. It seems like it takes a lot more time to get out than it did to come in. I'm drenched in sweat and take big swallows of water from my CamelBak. It feels much lighter.

When Ezra first gave me this CamelBak, it was too heavy for me and I complained about it. In fact, I didn't even want it. "You'll get used to it. It'll make you stronger." He was right. Now, even when it's full, I hardly notice it.

Back on the bus, I slump against the window, my temple leaving sweat on the glass. It's gross, I know, but I don't care right now. "We didn't find anything remotely like a prairie dog." I sit upright and wipe off my head. "Even if we did, people don't care about them. I think it's time to quit."

Carter takes out his phone and presses a button. "Poop."

I think he's saying poop as a substitute for darn, then realize he's talking about actual scat. "Oh, yeah. Let's look it up." I take out my phone. Normally I monitor how much data I use, so I don't go over, but today I decide not to check. Dana can pay the fees if she wants to move us.

We both start searching. Long, thin poop but only a couple inches. "Pine marten?" Carter says.

"A marten is a kind of weasel."

So we look up weasel poops.

And what we come up with are ferrets.

"What kind of ferrets are wild?" I ask the phone.

"Domestic ferrets do not live in the wild. But there is a wild species called the black-footed ferret (Mustela nigripes). *This species is endangered because its primary diet has dwindled due to habitat loss."*

Carter and I look at each other and grin.

I remember how during the meeting about Hedges, they talked about endangered animals. For the first time in a long time, hope fills me up from the inside out, and I feel as if I might float away on a bunch of balloons.

I open my notebook to the checklist and write a new note.

Find the black-footed ferret.

CHAPTER
22

I'm hunting through my cupboards for a treat I can take to Silas. Dana says the artists always get lonely and bored, so when they're here, we try to stop by with something. Maybe that's all that's wrong with Silas— he's lonely.

Yesterday, after we found the ferret, I emailed the footprint photos and poop photos to Myra right away to ask if it could be true. I haven't heard back yet. I wonder if she is avoiding answering, because she's going to tell me it's impossible. I mean, it probably doesn't feel good to crush the hopes and dreams of a child over and over. I consider sending her another email telling her I can take it, but instead decide to wait. Maybe she's busy.

All we have in the snack cupboard are healthy things, like sunflower seeds and dried fruit and brown rice cakes. Dana and I mostly eat fruit as a snack. There's an unopened package of unsulfured dried Turkish apricots.

I'm not sure what unsulfured means, but it sounds fancy. Silas seems like the type of person who would appreciate fruit over cookies anyway. I put that in my backpack along with my folder of photos.

I take the shuttle to the Grotto picnic area. Today there's a different driver named Marv, who has white hair, thick glasses, and grunts at everyone. He's no Felipe, and he drives so fast that the bus feels like some kind of snake we're riding on.

"I wish he would slow down," I hear someone say in Spanish, and I'm proud of myself for knowing that.

Silas's car is parked in front of the cabin, but nobody answers when I knock. Maybe he went on a hike. I take the trail to the lodge. It's a half mile, an easy walk, and crowded with people.

The trail is set against the canyon wall. To the right, as you walk, the land alternates between fields and hillsides dotted with trees, and then always the road beyond.

Today there's a herd of mule deer. These deer are always hanging out near this trail, along with turkeys, and today's no different. Myra told me that once she put a tracker on a deer from each group she knew about in the park. Each group went in a one-mile radius, moving from one spot to the next and then coming back. So these are different than the deer by the Pa'rus Trail.

A bunch of tourists are stopped both on the trail and the road on the other side of the field, taking photos.

Five cars are backed up, parked illegally, and one man opens his car door exactly as a bicyclist is going by. The bicyclist swerves in a wide semicircle.

"Watch it!" the bicyclist yells.

"You watch it," the tourist shouts. Not all tourists are nice. Most are, but not all of them. I've seen people climb over fences, litter, and sneak small, non-therapy dogs onto trails where they let them poop all over the place.

I guess I can maybe see why Dana wants to leave.

Ezra told Dana that no matter where she worked, there would be things she didn't like. "My university switched to the quarter system. Nobody likes it. But if I worked for a private company, there'd be policy decisions I disagreed with," he had said on his last visit. They were hanging out in our yard in folding camp chairs, watching the changing colors on the canyon walls as the sun went down.

Now I wonder if she had told him she was thinking of leaving.

I get to the lodge, making my way through crowds coming out of the adjoining café. The lodge is the second-oldest structure in Zion, after the artist cabin, and looks like a typical mountain lodge made of timber, with a porch in front. People are playing Frisbee or sitting on blankets on the wide lawn, admiring the views. Behind the building, the canyon walls rise up dramatically. In the winter, the tops of these peaks are often dotted with snow, even if the snow melts down here, and lo and behold, in one of the rocking chairs on the porch is Silas. On his phone. I run the last few feet up to him, my backpack bouncing. "Hey!"

"It's a Wednesday! I expected to see you yesterday." It's a joke, but the smile doesn't quite reach his eyes.

"Ha ha. I've never heard that one before." I sit next to him and unzip my pack, taking out the bag of dried apricots. "Here. They're unsulfured. I think those are better for you."

"Thanks," Silas says. "I do need more fiber. My system's been clogging up." He pats his tummy. He's got Instagram open on his phone, a photograph of what looks like Japan on it.

"Speaking of poop." I open the photo on my phone and show it to him.

"Ew, Tuesday. I don't need to see your digestive process."

"It's not *my* poop, Silas. It's from an animal." I go through the whole story, from when I took the photos to developing them to the poop.

He shuffles through the photos again and again. "If you could find the actual ferret, the case would be much stronger. It could even save Hedges."

Doesn't he know we thought of that? "Obviously. But I haven't yet." I swallow, feeling panicked as I remember they're tearing up land near that very spot as we speak. "And those are definitely endangered."

"Hmmm." He looks down at his phone. The photo is of a man standing under a blossoming cherry tree, a pond and a golden pavilion in the background.

"Thinking of going to Japan?"

He shakes his head. "No. I went last year. I took this photo." Silas holds up his phone. "That's my ex, Kyle." His purses his lips. "It feels weird to say that. Ex."

The man is smiling. I peer closer. A four-by-five camera is on a tripod next to him. My camera, now. "That's KM?"

Silas nods. "He filed for divorce two months ago."

"Oh." That explains why Silas seems depressed sometimes. I add "Sorry" as an afterthought.

"I wasn't expecting it at all. I wanted to make it work. He didn't. The end." He smiles bitterly. "It takes two to tango."

"You were dancers?"

"Ha. No. That's an expression." He looks into the distance, his eyes a little misty. "I thought coming here would be healing for me. But I keep coming back to this." He clicks on the screen, goes to Instagram, and brings up a photo of Kyle with another man. "He's already moved on." He sounds angry now, his hand clenching the phone until his knuckles turn white.

"Oof. That must be tough." I don't know what else

to say. I've never broken up with someone. Nor have I ever had a partner. I don't know what it's like. I focus on a fact-based question. "Is that why you were throwing away the camera?"

He nods. "I bought it for him. He said I could have it back, but I didn't want it."

And that's how it ended up in the trash. Silas was mad, like Dana said. I try to think of something Uncle Ezra would say, but nothing comes to mind. Instead, I think of my mother and how she's stuck. Silas is stuck, too, in a different way. Like a glitch that makes a DVD keep repeating the same scene.

Then Ezra's voice does come into my head, and without thinking, I blurt it out. "The only way to end something is to go through it."

Silas blinks. "What?"

Ezra actually said this in relation to a time we went hiking, and I wanted to stop—not because it was too high, but because I thought it was hard. Once I kind of accepted that it was difficult but knew I could take lots of breaks, I finished the hike and was glad I hadn't stopped. Now I take a moment and consider why I said it at all. "You can't keep thinking about him and how you were wronged. You'll never get through it that way."

"I'm trying."

I scratch my neck. "I don't know what you're doing, but it's not working."

He laughs. "I love how unapologetically blunt you are, Tuesday."

"Unapologetic? Why should people apologize for saying what's true? For example"—I nod at his phone—"stalking him on Instagram seems like a bad idea."

"You're right." He shakes his head. "I came to the lodge to post my stuff." Silas taps the screen, going back to his own account.

I wonder if Silas will be able to get over his ex while he's here, or if he believes what I said was helpful. Dana says there's only so much you can do for another person. "How many followers do you have?"

"A couple thousand. It's a way to get people interested in my work." He jiggles his knee.

I take out my prints. "I need to post some more on my account."

"Oh, yeah. Let's see yours." He looks at my KeepZionDark account. "Jeez, look at that follower count!"

"No way!" It's actually 920.

"Oh! You're mentioned in Lyla Redding's story." He shows me. She reposted the photo that Carter tagged her in to her own account, to the parts that only show for a day. "That's why."

LOVE ZION, Lyla wrote. I wonder if she even remembers us. Well, she doesn't know my name—and I don't have my photo up on my Instagram profile or anything. "I don't think it means anything." These people who followed us likely won't pay attention to anything else I post. "They're probably all bots anyway. There are a ton of those on these social media sites."

Silas tells me it's not enough to post pictures. "You should do videos. Live sessions."

I make a gagging noise. "No, thank you."

"It builds an audience. That's how social media works. You want people to know about Hedges, don't you?"

"That sounds like a lot of effort, and not the kind of thing I like to do. But I'll ask Carter. He likes social media." I take out my notebook and write down, *Do Instagram live feeds (Carter)*.

"But you know more about the technical stuff," Silas says. "What if you did a photography tutorial? Or a tour of Hedges?"

"The signal's not very strong there. I don't think I can do a live thing."

Silas sighs. "Just think about it, Ms. Negativity."

"I'm not negative. I'm realistic. There's a difference." I squint at him. "Anyway, you're one to talk. Why aren't you this positive about getting over your breakup?"

"Ouch," Silas says. "And true."

chapter 23

After I leave Silas, I take the tram to the museum, then walk down the hill to the science offices. Dana's car is there. Myra's Subaru Outback is not. This makes me feel better about the fact that Myra hasn't answered her email.

Sure enough, Dana's back in her office, sitting on the bouncy ball she has in there. I say hello to her and come inside. "Hey, Tuesday." Dana doesn't look up. "How are you?"

"Just here to use Wi-Fi." I sit in her chair.

I have an email from the ClearNights forum. I feel a little guilty, because only a couple weeks ago my goal was to find a new comet and I've barely used my telescope at all since then.

It's CheddarBunny, aka Natalia. *Check out this photo of Jupiter I got.* It's beautiful and shows the storms.

Normally when you take a photograph from Earth with a camera, it's pretty much black and white. You can put a photo into Photoshop and make it colored. She makes hers into art.

Amazing, I respond, because it is. Making art out of planet photos is something I never thought of doing before. I mean, I've seen it done but I never wanted to do it before now. "Can we get Photoshop?" I ask Dana.

"Maybe. It's a monthly subscription. I'll have to see if it's in the budget." Dana doesn't ask why I need it. "We'll see."

Carter says that when his parents say, "We'll see," it means no. Dana always means that she needs more information.

Another message from CheddarBunny appears. *You watching the Bootids?* The meteor shower.

You know it, I respond. That's next week. I never miss it. It's the time of year Ezra always came to visit us, too, because he had all summer off.

Dana clicks away on her keyboard. "So have you seen Carter lately?"

"Yesterday. We did a hike."

"Where?"

I hesitate. Dana's never told me specifically I can't go to Hedges, but I've always known it requires permissions to go beyond the rock-climbing area. Dana's never told me that I can't take the bus to St. George, and I wouldn't do that, either.

I didn't go alone, but I have the feeling I went beyond what I'm allowed to do. I don't want to tell her and have to explain myself even more.

However, we already emailed the poop photos to Myra, so she's going to find out sooner or later. I take a deep breath. "We went to Hedges. And look what I found." I show her the photos on my phone. "Poop that I've never seen before!"

"You went to Hedges?" Her voice rises.

"Never mind that." I shake the phone. "This is important! If this is what I think it is, it'll be worth it."

She takes it and squints. "What kind of animal is that from? It's so odd. It looks like a wire!"

"Good question. Carter and I believe it is a black-footed ferret."

"Oh." Dana hands the phone back. "I've never seen one of those."

"That's because they're endangered." She doesn't get it. "That means the new owners would have to stop construction."

"Did you see it?"

"No." I cross my arms.

"Then how do you know it's not some other animal?" Dana asks.

"Because there were footprints, too. Carter has those photos."

"Did you email Myra?"

"Yes, of course." I can't keep the indignant note out of my voice. "What do you think I am?"

"Let's wait to see what Myra says." Dana bounces on her ball the way she does when she's thinking. "If it's significant, she'll take care of it. But I don't want you going to Hedges without me or an authorized person. Period."

"What are you talking about? I've been in there plenty of times." I click on another photo of Jupiter. This is what I was worried about. That I shouldn't go in.

"You always go in there with me. The general public is only allowed in as far as the bouldering school. You're not allowed to go beyond."

"That's silly. Uncle Ezra took me in, too."

"Uncle Ezra and I knew the old owners, Tuesday," Dana says firmly. "I'm the archaeologist so, yes, the rules are a little more lax for me because I have that position. The new owners don't want you back there. It's a liability issue. If something happened, they would be in big trouble. Not to mention, I don't want you getting hurt."

I frown.

"Promise me you won't go back there again."

"I can't do that," I say. "Because I'm going to go back there with you."

Dana frowns back at me. We have the same double lines between our eyebrows. "Tuesday," she says warningly. "You know what I mean."

"Okay," I say. "I won't go back there without an extremely good reason and permission from an authority figure."

"Good." She turns away. "Maybe you ought to think about being a lawyer. You find a lot of loopholes."

"Uncle Ezra always said there were too many lawyers."

"That's only because his ex was one," Dana says drily.

She made a joke about Ezra! This seems like a good time to bring up the poem. She's talking about her brother but not being too emotional about it. "I think we should do his ashes. Please look at the poem with me."

She bounces up and down and starts typing. "I'll do those when I'm ready, Tuesday. I have to get back to work now."

And that is that.

CHAPTER

24

The next week, it's already mid-June and time for the Bootid meteor shower. Myra still hasn't responded. I sent her another email in case she missed the first, because Dana says the biologists were busy with bighorn lambs and things, but she didn't answer that. I try to focus on the meteors instead, promising myself if Myra doesn't answer by the end of tomorrow, I'll find her in person.

The funny thing about meteor showers is they can be predicted every year. There are even calendars you can look at to see when they all are. In June, in this hemisphere, it's Bootid.

Meteor showers are nothing but comet dust. A comet passes over and sheds meteors like a cat sheds fur. That's why they're so predictable, because comets are so predictable.

I walk over to the administration building, connect

to the internet, and I post another photo. I look at the follower count. It's actually dropped since I looked at it last—now there are only eight hundred or so. I knew they were a bunch of bots.

Cool photo, someone wrote.

I love hoodoos! I saw them all over Utah.

Hey, your account is great. Be a brand ambassador for our company!

That one isn't a real comment. I delete it.

Poor quality.

It's sad that someone took time out of their day to write something mean when they could be doing something more productive. Anyway, if I don't look at troll comments, it's pretty much like those people don't exist. Ezra said that giving trolls attention is like giving fire oxygen. "If you extinguish the oxygen, Tuesday, then the fire goes out." He knew this because sometimes people would leave him comments on social media or on his website. He didn't care.

If I find a comet, I'm naming it after Ezra.

I think again about his poem and the ashes. If Carter's right, and he's telling me where to put his ashes, I'm going to need my mother to help. But how can we solve the puzzle together if she won't even talk about it?

The botanists are walking by. "Hey, Tuesday!" Megan calls. "We're looking for sage seeds. Want to help?"

Nick looks into the sky as if there's something interesting up there, even though it's clear blue without even a bird in sight. I almost say no, but I'm not doing anything else. "Okay," I say. "Why not?"

I walk knee-deep in the brush. Megan's given me some rubber gloves, and I'm looking for sage flowers that have lost their purply tints and turned to mottled gray-browns, ready to give up their seeds. I shake some gently into a plastic bag. "What are you going to do with these?"

"Regrow them in places where habitats need to be restored," Megan replies. "Remember, get one or two flowers off each plant. We need them to regerminate here, too."

I accidentally reach for the same plant as Nick. "After you," I say.

"It's fine. After you."

I step back, though, and finally he shrugs and gets the seeds.

"Why does it bug you that I think I'm smart?" I ask him.

He jumps. "Um, I . . ."

"I heard you talking that one day," I inform him. "Voices carry more than you think in a canyon."

He swallows. "It's that . . . Well. You're always telling us about the stars."

I think that's a very odd reason. "Just because I know

a lot about the stars doesn't mean I know about other things," I point out. "I don't know much about plants. And I know more about Magic: The Gathering than you do because I've played it more and I like that kind of thing."

He straightens now and looks me in the eye. "It's the *way* you say it. Like we're all boneheads because we don't know, too."

I swallow. That's how I sound? "I thought I was telling you in a matter-of-fact manner."

"That's not how it comes across." He shrugs. "Look, it's fine. You're a kid, and I shouldn't get annoyed with you."

I turn to another bush, heat stinging my cheeks as a hot dry breeze rattles the grasses around us. Last time I didn't say anything when Nick said something like this and let it bother me on and on. I could let it go. What does it matter what Nick thinks? In a month he'll return to whatever state he's from and I'll never see him again.

But I want to be heard. "I don't know how to *not* talk like that. It's just me. That's how I talk. I don't think you're unintelligent." I pause. "Except about Magic: The Gathering."

Nick laughs. "Okay, Tuesday. We can be friends. Deal?" He sticks out his hand.

I look down at it. "Deal." He pumps it up and down until my arm's like spaghetti.

Megan comes back, and I realize she's been giving us distance. "Way to stand up for yourself," she whispers. I nod. I don't need her encouragement, and if she hadn't said anything, I would still be fine, but I'm glad for it.

My phone buzzes. An email. I open it. Myra, finally! Please, please, let me be right.

This does look like some kind of weasel poop, Myra writes. *That's interesting. Can you show me where you found it? I'm available tomorrow afternoon.*

Yes, I type.

Finally something good. Tomorrow I'll be able to check another item off my list. Things are looking up.

CHAPTER
25

That evening, Dana and I pull into the south parking lot to see the meteor shower. The lot is by the nature center building and the south campground. It's almost full, but Dana finally finds a spot at the far end. "These things get more crowded every year," she grumbles, and I agree. We spray ourselves with bug repellent and head over to the field.

Dana's phone pings. This area has good reception. "Text from Myra," she says. "She says that you can show her where you saw the droppings. Tomorrow."

"But why'd she text you?"

"She would need my permission either way. It doesn't matter."

It does matter, a little. It tells me Myra doesn't 100 percent take me seriously. "Okay."

People swarm all over the meadow, talking loudly, not being careful where they point their flashlights. One shines right into my face, and I hold my hands up. "Hey!" I say sharply. "Don't you know it takes the human eye like an hour to get back to being able to see in the dark? Turn off those lights!"

But it's as if I shouted into a pillow, because zero people pay attention to me. I need a horn to get their attention.

"This is kind of awful," Dana yells to me as we get jostled between a family with toddlers and a group of long-bearded men wearing motorcycle vests. She hates crowds as much as I do. I can't stand the thought that someday Hedges will be exactly the same as this.

"Agreed," I yell back, because otherwise she can't hear me.

In the middle I spot Melody, the park's astronomer, and tug Dana over to her.

"Tuesday! Dana! Thanks for coming." Melody's set up her medium-size telescope. She sighs. "I didn't expect this much of a turnout."

"It's going to take forever to get a turn," I note.

"Want me to help you corral everyone?" Dana asks.

"No. I've got it. But thanks."

"Is this where the booty shower is?" a voice behind me asks.

It's Silas. Of course. Making one of his jokes. "Silas!"

"Enjoying your stay?" Dana asks politely, like everyone always does. And like always, Silas nods.

"It's so beautiful." He winces as someone steps on his foot. "Except for the hordes of people."

I look at Dana. She looks at me with a raised brow. "Want to go somewhere else?"

"East side?" I ask.

"Better." She looks at Silas. "You in?"

"In like Flynn," Silas says, whatever that means.

I suspect I know where we're heading as soon as we leave the park, and I'm correct. Dana drives us into Hedges.

"I thought the public wasn't allowed back here." Silas cranes his head as he tries to see into the darkness. "Boy. It's pitch black."

"Exactly," I say.

"I'm not the public," Dana says.

"You fancy," Silas says.

"That's correct. I am." Dana pulls over and parks, and we get out the gear. I turn on the red headlamp. "We're going to go up a little higher, Tuesday," Dana says. "Are you comfortable with that?"

"Sort of," Silas says.

"I was talking to Tuesday. But are you afraid of heights?"

"A tad. But I'll be okay." Silas sounds fake-brave.

"It's all right if you want to turn back," I tell him. "Dana and I won't be mad."

"And miss a once-in-a-lifetime event? No way."

"It happens every year," I tell him.

"Still. Next year I won't be here in Zion. Heck, maybe I won't be here at all. I can't tell the future." Silas is joking, but I see my mother's shoulders clench and know she's thinking of Ezra.

Dana turns on her red headlamp and leads us up a trail. It's not anywhere I've been before. "Stay to the right so you don't fall off."

"Right." Silas creeps along. I've never hiked with someone who's more scared of heights than I am. Or if they were, they didn't say they were. Silas's breathing gets rapid and loud, and he slows down even more. I'm paying so much attention to him that I forget that I was ever frightened. My mother, unaware of how slow he's going, gets ahead of us.

"Dana, wait!" I call. She stops and turns around. "He needs help."

She hurries back down the trail, her boots crunching but her steps confident, like a bighorn sheep. Her light shines on his face. He's all sweaty and pale, squinting against the headlamp. "We can turn around if you want," she says gently. "We can look at the sky from the car."

Silas opens an eye to look at Dana, then me. "No, no. If it's the best spot, then I want to see it."

"Okay." She holds out her hand to me. "You doing all right, Tuesday?"

"I'm fine." Trails aren't a problem—it's boulders. And I've done one of those. "I would also be fine if we went back."

"I'm good." Silas swallows so loud I can hear it, like a raindrop falling into a bucket of water. "Let's go."

We keep going up, the trail getting so steep that I'm leaning all the way forward and every step feels like I'm doing a deep squat, my knee coming up almost against my stomach. "How long is it? Five miles?" Silas asks.

"It's only a half mile total. Not much farther!" Dana says, and then we round the corner and suddenly come to a small flat plateau of sandy rock. A few stubby piñon trees dot the surface. Otherwise it kind of looks like Mars.

"Stay close to this boulder." Dana points. "There's quite a drop-off."

"You don't need to tell me twice." Silas sets down the telescope and shakes his hands out. "I was gripping this so hard I lost feeling!"

"Thanks for carrying it," Dana says. "Tuesday, can you spread out the tarp here?"

I put out the blanket where she's pointing, then set up the telescope. I sit down and crane my head back, watching the blinking and fluttering lights. A meteor blazes against the backdrop of the Milky Way like a flashbulb going off. "I saw one!" You don't even need a telescope to watch a meteor shower, because you can't see the whole sky at once. But it's nice to have in case we want to see a detail.

"I did, too!" Silas sits next to me. He puts his hand against the sky, his fingers splayed out. "Wow. It looks like I can touch the stars."

"You can't. They're very far away." I open my backpack and take out a granola bar. "You should turn off your headlamp."

"I know . . ." He trails off, and I realize he was joking and he realizes I take things literally. I think. He turns off his light.

Dana sits down by me. I'm looking around, remembering something, and my heart double-skips. "Is this where Ezra tried to take me that one time, when I wouldn't climb?"

"That place was even higher. It was where he and I went once, when I worked here for the summer, a long time ago. When I was pregnant with you," Dana says. "It involved a little boulder scrambling. I don't know why he tried to take you there at night." She sounds a little annoyed, as if her brother is still alive for her to be mad at.

"He probably wanted her to see the best possible place," Silas says. My eyes have adjusted, and I can see both their faces in the starlight. For a second, I'm reminded of being together with Ezra and Dana. A sort of family feeling. It's both comfortable and strange, because of course it's Silas and not my uncle.

"Yeah, he did," I respond to Silas. "He always wanted to push me like that."

"He sounds great," Silas says. "I bet you miss him a lot."

I picture Ezra here, watching the stars. He'd jump up and whoop at the meteors, as if they were players in some kind of cosmic football game instead of balls of rocks and flaming gases. "Yeah," I say, expecting to tear up. Instead, a dull, heavy longing settles down in my chest, and I don't try to push it away like I usually do. I let it sit there, knowing that sadness this big won't stay around forever, and I hug it to me like a teddy bear.

And I know it's not only about Ezra; it's about the development. At this time next year, all this will be gone. I mean, Dana and I might be gone, too, for all I know.

Dana sits there, her face as expressionless as a boulder. Is she feeling the same? Or maybe she's feeling nothing. I want her to do *something*, but I can't figure out what.

Then I realize—I want her to comfort me. Put her arm around me. When I was little, I stopped liking hugs. They felt suffocating. I didn't like the smells of the other person, the feeling of being controlled even though I know Dana didn't do it to control me. So Dana always respected that. It's another Tuesday quirk. I never hugged Ezra, but he never asked.

I think about the poem again. White socks, white socks. Owl wings. Another place, higher up. I swallow. "Dana, can you take me to the place where you and Ezra camped?" That might be it, I want to tell her. Where he wants you to put his ashes. If she says yes, then I'll tell her all that. I don't want her to shut down again, like she did at the diner. Like she always does.

"I don't even remember where it is." Her expression isn't visible in this light.

I turn away from her. Even though I can't see her face, I can tell a lie when I hear one.

26

Myra's Outback rattles as she drives me out of Zion, to Hedges. "I need to get this muffler fixed," she says.

Today Dana has her video interview with South Dakota. I kind of hope she messes it up, then feel guilty for thinking that. I want my mother to be happy, no matter what. "So you think it's a ferret?" I say to Myra, to get my mind off Dana.

"If it is a ferret, then you probably did see a prairie dog the other day." Myra turns into Hedges. "Prairie dogs are a ferret's primary diet. So when those went away, so did the ferrets."

That makes sense. "So this would be a really important discovery, then?" I ask hopefully.

"It would. If it's true. I need evidence. It could've been an animal with a bad tummy."

At the entrance, the vineyard is razed and the ground

completely level. From the model, I remember there being a wide entrance road with some kind of fountain in the middle. Which is not very natural.

We drive past the empty archaeological site. Then we park and walk in. "I have to be back for a meeting in an hour," Myra says. "So let's make it quick."

There's something new here. Backhoes and bulldozers and various construction people. A cold feeling hits my insides as I look up at the hill where they're working.

I think Carter was right. They're making a road.

Myra shows her identification to the construction people, and I lead her way back into the canyon. She glances around as we go through the slot canyon. "This feels more and more unlikely all the time."

"I mean, if you're an animal, there are other ways to get there," I point out.

Myra pushes her ranger hat back on her forehead. "Just show me where these things are."

Myra's getting annoyed. I go quiet and lead her to where I found the poop. Or where I think we saw the poop.

But today, there's no poop here. No footprints. Nothing. It's like Carter and I imagined it all.

"I could be wrong." I look around the area. It's generally where we were, but it's hard to say exactly. "I should've left a marker."

"Maybe it was a fluke." Myra looks at her watch. "Tuesday, I know you want the development to stop and so do I. But I'm wondering, was that prairie dog really there?"

"Really where?"

"In the photo."

My face goes hot as I understand what Myra is getting at. "I don't have Photoshop."

"It's easy to manipulate images." Myra bends to look into my face, her stare so intense it's like a physical slap. I glance at the ground. This probably makes her think I'm guilty, but all it means is I don't like that much eye contact.

"Ask Dana." My stomach twists. "Do you think I'm lying?"

She hesitates. "I *think* that Hedges is important to you."

"I'm not a liar." My voice rises.

"Okay."

"You think I put a prairie dog in the photo so I could say that . . . what . . . its predator is here, too? I didn't even know black-footed ferrets existed before this! Or that they ate prairie dogs!" What is she going to accuse me of next? "What kind of criminal mastermind do you think I am? I'm twelve years old."

"It's my job to be skeptical." Myra starts walking back. "Come on."

I trot after her. "I'm not some random person off the street," I say hotly. "I'm Tuesday Beals. Daughter of Dana Beals." The way I'm saying it makes me sound like I'm some kind of nobility in a fantasy novel. I'm glad she doesn't laugh at me. "I do not lie."

She twists her mouth down. "Your mom told me you and Carter snuck back here, so I think that, yes, sometimes you do what you want. You're a smart girl, and you use that to your advantage."

Why does it feel like people are using the word *smart* as an insult against me? I don't have anything else to say to her.

Myra and I don't talk on the way back. I try not to be mad at her. Myra's a good biologist, and a nice person, but it's her job to question things. To protect the park. If someone claimed they found an archaeological site, I tell myself, Dana would have to ask questions, too.

I look at my Instagram. Three hundred or so more followers—that's over a thousand now. More comments. *Somebody needs to step in and conserve the area*, someone writes. Not even any trolls this time. Carter's right. It's bringing attention to Zion. Besides, the thought of going home after this versus doing some work in the darkroom is no contest.

The four-by-five plates are safe in my backpack. "Actually," I say to Myra, "can you drop me off at the photography studio?"

CHAPTER
27

anielle helps me make the negatives, then the proofs, and drives me home. I don't tell her what Myra said about the prairie dog. I think it'd make her mad. Maybe Danielle would call my mother. Though Danielle could sure say that I didn't Photoshop anything.

I'm sitting outside the house when Dana gets home from work at six. I'm still mad and confused about what Myra said. I guess the fact that Carter and I went to Hedges without permission made her think we were up to something. I stand up as Dana gets out of the car, ready to tell her everything.

But before I can, Dana stops and puts her bag on a rock. She takes a breath. "Guess what?"

My stomach twists. I know what she's going to say. "You got the job."

She nods, and I can't tell if she's happy or not. "School starts in late August."

"I guess I don't get a say, do I?"

"This is what's best for both of us. It's time for us to move on. Soon this area will be overbuilt and be like every other place." Dana looks at me, her eyes anime big. "It won't matter."

I don't believe this. "So you're moving us to someplace that's already like that? No!"

"You'll get better schooling there. And the opportunity to meet new people, make new friends. In a place where it's easier to get around, where you can walk to someone's house after school."

She's making a good point, but still, my heart burns as if she literally stabbed me in the chest with a lightsaber. "I don't want to go. I'm fine with everything like it is here."

She stares at me for a moment, then lowers her eyes. "I'm sorry. This is what's best."

She doesn't sound sorry. It's the same kind of sorry adults use when they're telling you something negative, but they're not apologizing. I stare back at her. Though Dana's emotions seem to have turned off, all of mine have turned on at once. My ears fill with a roaring noise.

I take the poem out of my pocket. "You haven't even tried to solve his riddle. His ashes are just sitting in our house. How can we leave?"

"Tuesday, I know you don't want to hear this, but Uncle Ezra isn't going to mind what happens to his ashes." Dana's voice has a steel edge to it. She's in full scientist mode. That means she is leaving all emotion out of her thoughts and words. "That poem has nothing to do with anything!"

I hesitate. Am I wrong about this? I was wrong about it having to do with an archaeological site. Then I decide, no, I'm not. I can't be. Otherwise, nothing about his death makes sense. I just want this one thing to be true. "It has to be about something, Dana." I read it out loud again. I need her to talk about it with me. Talk about Ezra with me.

"I don't need to hear it!" she interrupts.

"Listen, Carter's dad and Danielle's husband both told people what to do with their ashes! Uncle Ezra did, too. It's so obvious. I'd solve it myself, but I can't. I need you."

She shakes her head stubbornly. "Let it go, Tuesday."

For a second, I wonder how it got so windy. Then I realize—it's the sound of my blood pumping by my ears because I'm so mad. My ear canals feel like they're on fire. I swallow, my throat dry. "I will never let it go."

Without waiting for her to respond, I turn and run down the road.

"Where are you going?" she yells.

I get on the shuttle and ride it toward the back of the park, passing the place where people used to store food thousands of years ago, passing Silas's cabin, passing everything. At the end of the road, the shuttle stops, and I follow the others out, walking with the crowd of tourists on the paved trail to the Narrows.

The Narrows was something that Ezra and Dana and I were supposed to do this summer. It's a hard hike because it's through the Virgin River—you have to get a permit and wear waterproof gear, and it takes about eight hours.

The trail back to that entrance is about a mile long. On the right the canyon wall rises. It's shady and cool here even in the hottest part of the afternoon, because the canyon runs north and south. In parts the walls are covered in moss. This is where the natural waterfalls form whenever it rains, and drip for days afterward. I put my hand on the rock. It seems to breathe out cool air like a living creature hunkered down in the canyon. If living things breathed cold air instead of warm.

Below the trail is an open area dotted with trees, and then the white bank of the Virgin. It's wide here, still that green-clear color, and this area has a lot of rocks that make the shooshing noise even louder. On the other side of the river is more sandstone canyon wall, blocking out most of the blue sky.

I think about making my way into the Narrows. It's nice today, still ninety-five degrees even now. There's not a cloud in the sky, so it would be okay for me to slosh my way a little bit into the trail, I reason. I could follow one of these groups. A lot of people don't bother with the dry suits in the summer, when the water's warmer. I want to walk back there until the walls close around me. Until the sky disappears.

Even though I want to go back there, I remember Ezra's warnings. Always hike with a buddy. "You never know when you can trip and break a bone," he says. "You don't carry an emergency kit because you're *planning* on an emergency. They happen out of nowhere."

So going there alone isn't a good idea. If something happened to me I'd have to depend on a stranger to help, which might not happen.

Instead I veer off and head toward the river. The cottonwood trees' roots all seem like they're reaching out for the water, like hands trying to scoop out candy from a Halloween bucket. From here, back the way I came, there's a view of the Great White Throne, the sunshine making the white rock at the top bright like new paper, rising above the jagged edge of Angels Landing. I've seen this view dozens of times, but I've never paid attention to it quite like this. I wish I'd brought my camera.

I run down the steep dirt path and find a tree near the bend. This is where Carter and I liked to play during picnics, making a fort inside this tree as our parents chatted nearby.

I plop into the loose white sand. Some little kids play

not far away, wading into the river and shrieking, their mother and father standing close by, ready to grab them.

I stick my hands into the ground, feeling the grains close around me. I think about how ancient this sand is. How millions of years ago it was a dune and then it was sandstone like the walls of the canyon, until the river cut it away. I think about the ancient people who walked along the river like we are now, leaving behind their pottery shards for Dana to find.

A little girl shrieks as the man picks her up and swings her. "Unkie Noah!" she yells. "Higher, higher!"

So the man's her uncle, not her father. A shudder runs through me and I wish Ezra were here, too.

Because I had Ezra, I'd never missed not having a father. And now I don't have anyone like that. I only have my mother, who will barely talk to me about him and who doesn't care what I think about anything.

I've never felt so all alone in the world.

I draw my legs up into my chest and put my head on them, letting my hair fall over my face. I'm crying, awful ugly sobs that seem like they're getting torn out of me. My ribs shake. *Ezra, Ezra, Ezra.*

It's so unfair.

Someone touches me gently on the shoulder. "Are you all right?" It's the uncle, the woman standing right behind him, the little girl clutching his hand.

I lift my head and wipe the bleary tears out of my

eyes. "I'm okay. Thanks."

"Where are your parents?" the woman asks.

I draw myself up straighter. I don't want her calling anyone. "I'm a park kid. My mom works here. I'm authorized."

"Authorized to do what?" the uncle asks. Usually people accept that I say I'm authorized.

"To go wherever," I answer, and then, to explain my crying, add, "My uncle died."

"I'm so sorry," the man says, and he does sound sorry, which makes me start crying a little all over again.

I nod, not wanting to lose it in front of strangers, and I get up and start following the river back toward the offices. "Me too."

I trudge along the river. You can walk the whole way back if you try, but it's something like six miles. I plan to go until my legs get tired and then catch the shuttle. I've only gotten to Weeping Rock, right next to the Narrows, when I hear thudding footsteps.

"Tuesday!" It's Carter. He runs up to me, his hair flying backward. "I was so worried."

"Why?" I sniffle.

"Your mom came looking for you and said you'd run off." He gestures at the sky. "It'll be dark soon."

"So what? The shuttles run until eight thirty in the summer."

"Still. Why did you run off?"

I shake my head, still unable to say the words. "I am leaving the park. There is probably no ferret and Myra thinks I made it up. This place will be ruined.

"My uncle is dead and I won't ever see him again, and my mother won't even do what he wants with his ashes."

It's too much to blast at Carter. I stare at the ground. "Carter," I say slowly. "Will you and I really always be friends?"

"Of course. I've already said that." He sounds indignant, like I did when Myra suggested I had photoshopped the animal.

I look at his face. With Carter, what you see is what you get. He never tries hiding anything. "Just making sure."

"My mom's waiting in Delilah." Carter peers into my eyes. "Do you want a ride?"

I nod.

CHAPTER

28

Dana's on the front step, chewing on her fingernail. She jumps up as Jenny stops at our house. "Thanks!" she calls.

"No problem," Jenny says.

I get out and trudge over to my mother, my feet kicking up dirt clouds. Jenny and Carter drive away.

Dana peers into my face. "You had me worried."

I shrug with one shoulder.

"We'll talk about it later." She nods at the house. "I made dinner. Then how about some gin rummy?"

"I'm not in the mood." I'm probably never going to tell her about Myra and the Photoshop thing. In fact, I may never tell Dana about anything, ever again. Not if she's going to make me feel bad about confiding stuff. I go inside, wash up, then get a plate of food—some kind of chopped salad—and shut myself inside my room.

* * *

I have trouble sleeping, waking up over and over again, thoughts of the park and moving and Instagram running through my head. Will all our new followers amount to anything? Also, I'm hot. Finally, at about three, I give up and go outside. I creep out the back door.

The stars twinkle like nothing bad is happening. Everything is the same.

The air out here is cooler than inside but still humid. I catch a whiff of campfire—it smells like someone's burning piñon, like spicy pine sap. I get an idea to make a video for Instagram and point my phone camera at the sky. "Can you see all the stars?" I ask in a low voice. An owl hoots in a tree nearby, and the dark shape of a bat flaps across the sky. "When Hedges is built up, this won't be visible. Not like this, anyway.

"Did you know that different planets are visible depending on the time of evening and which month it is?" I say. "Today I can see Saturn almost dead south, and Jupiter up and to the right." I point my phone in that direction. It probably doesn't look all that great, but they get the idea.

An owl hoots and calls. A mosquito lands on my arm, and I swat it. I won't miss that. But they probably have mosquitoes in South Dakota.

No. I won't let myself think about leaving as if it's going to happen.

Uncle Ezra warned me to watch out for magical

thinking. "That's how people trick themselves into believing that things they don't like aren't true," he said. "Or because they can't wrap their minds around it. Like the Earth being flat or that global warming doesn't exist."

There's no conspiracy of scientists. Scientists are competitive, and they try to argue each other's research out of existence all the time.

"Data," I say out loud. I don't have any data for South Dakota—not a real moving date, not even the official job offer letter. Until then I don't have to believe it.

I go back to bed and pull up my sheets, a tiny bit comforted.

CHAPTER
29

Maybe because I was looking at the stars, I dream about Ezra.

In the dream, I'm on a high cliff with him, but it's not in Zion. It's somewhere I haven't been, but for some reason, I know where I am—the Badlands. It reminds me of Zion, all rocky canyons, but the colors are more uniform, bands of red and green and white repeating each other exactly from hill to hill, as if someone colored them all in at once and then removed the canyon parts.

Usually, in dreams, you don't know it's not real, but somehow I know I'm dreaming. Ezra sits next to me, staring out at the landscape, a little smile on his face as if he's thinking of a secret. He's so close I can see the pores on his nose, the sweat on his brow, the brown hairs on his arm that he said made him part ape. One leg is stretched out before him, and the other is drawn up, his arm resting on his knee. I recognize the blanket we're sitting on, a waterproof camping one that Ezra used. He smells like campfire and popcorn, and I know we must have made popcorn like we always do—with loose kernels and a little oil in a covered pan over the fire.

I'm amazed at how much more my sleeping self can remember than my waking self.

I touch his arm—it feels just like him. Ezra looks at me. "What a view, eh?"

I swallow. "You're dead. What are you doing here?"

His brow wrinkles, puzzled. "What are you talking about? I'm sitting right by you."

"But this is a dream." I squeeze his arm, and now it's squishier, and I understand I'm touching my blanket, not him—I'm about to wake up and I don't want to. "You died last year."

He smiles sadly. "You're right. I'm not on Earth any-more, but I'm still with you."

I think of the ashes. "Because we haven't put you in your final resting place?"

He squints. "That would help." A cat appears, wind-ing through his legs, purring. It's the black-and-white cat from their childhood photo.

"Are you saying you're a ghost and you're haunting me? Because you believe in science."

"I am a ghost," he answers, "but only figuratively speaking. I'm not a literal ghost haunting you. I'm pushing at your subconscious until things get settled."

This sounds so much like Ezra.

"I don't know how to settle things," I say, and the poem appears in my hand. I can't read the words. "Tell me what you meant."

"You can figure it out, Tuesday. You're the smartest niece I have."

"I'm your only niece."

"Whatever you need." He gently taps my forehead with a finger. "Is here."

I shake my head, tears forming. "It's not! Ezra, I've messed up everything. I followed the wrong clues. I still can't save Hedges, and I don't even know where to put your ashes."

The cat meows and rubs against my legs. I'm amazed at how real it feels. There are even little pieces of fur left behind. "You haven't, Tuesday. You have to learn to be okay with uncertainty. That's all life is. Nobody is guaranteed anything."

I glare at him. I want him to tell me everything will be fine. That I'll be happy in South Dakota or, if we stay in Zion, that I'll be happy here even if Hedges is a whole new town. "That is not very reassuring."

"So you might as well hope for the best. Have some faith in that which you cannot see."

I smile a little. "Now you sound like a Jedi." Which is also so Ezra.

Ezra laughs. "Perhaps that's what I've become."

Then I wake up. I've probably watched too many *Star Wars* movies where the Jedi master returns from the dead to tell their students important things. That's why I dreamed about him.

But my brain and my body feel like I just saw him. And the black-and-white cat felt so real. The mind is so interesting. Maybe I'll be a neuroscientist.

After I have breakfast, I walk over to Carter's. I should tell him about South Dakota—it feels weird not telling him. Is not telling someone something important a lie? I think it is, from my jittery stomach.

Carter's not home, but I take the opportunity to use his Wi-Fi and upload my video about the stars to Instagram TV. Adding content, like Silas said to. I do have some more followers—about a dozen more. *Great work!* says PhotobuffNewZealand.

And someone has shared my work on their account. It's CheddarBunny, my friend Natalia from Texas. *Important: Keep Zion Dark*, she writes.

Thanks, I type.

In the distance, I think I can hear the roar of construction equipment back in Hedges, bordering the park. I hope it's my imagination, but I don't think it is.

I sit on a boulder and open my notebook. *How to get Dana to talk about Ezra*, I write on a fresh page.

Demand to see a therapist
Lock her in a room and don't let her leave

I sigh. I can't make anyone do anything.

A blue car drives by with a bunch of cardboard in the back. Silas. "Hey, Tuesday!"

"Where are you going?" I ask.

"I'm going to recycle this, and then I'm going to paint," he says.

"Where?"

"Probably right here." He gestures. "Watchman. I've done it before, but I've run out of places."

I nod to be polite. I can't count the number of art pieces I've seen of this peak.

"What?" he asks. "Too boring?"

"Watchman. Everyone does that."

"Everyone has painted everything already." He wipes his brow.

That's true, like Carter had said about the stories.

"Whatcha got there?"

I flip back. "It's a poem my uncle wrote while he was sick. I think they're instructions."

"Instructions for what?"

"For what to do with his ashes. Like a scavenger hunt. I think." I hand it over.

"Really?" He shakes his head and reads the poem out loud. "Why would he leave you a riddle?"

"I don't know. But he liked doing things like that."

"He sounds like he was a fun guy."

"I think you would have been friends," I say, suddenly absolutely certain they would have been, as sure as I am that when I look to the north I'll see Venus. Even though Ezra was twenty years older than Silas, they would have made jokes together and talked about everything. My chest seems to crack open like a fissure, forming a canyon. "I know you would."

Silas gives me a curious little smile, then reads the poem.

At the place beyond the meadows
On the table where we ate
In white socks we used to roam

"Hmm," Silas says. "What's this thing about white socks?"

"I'm not sure. I was thinking it had something to do with where we went camping, because we didn't have shoes on in the tent." I shrug.

Silas hands the poem back. "What did your mom say?"

I shrug.

"Nothing?"

"She didn't want to talk about it," I say at last. For some reason, admitting this to Silas makes me feel . . .

ashamed. As if my mother has failed me. But I don't know how.

"Oh." He smiles ruefully. "I get that."

"You do?"

He nods. "She's not ready."

I stare past him at the mountains. In the summer sun, they seem to glow as if they're being heated from the inside out. "I don't know if she'll ever be ready," I say at last.

"It sounds like she didn't mourn him fully. Like she needs to process her grief."

I think about this, how she didn't cry, how she refuses to talk about this. "How do I get her to do that?"

"You can't. She has to want to." He wipes more sweat off his forehead. "I think doing something with his ashes would help her have closure. If you can get her to."

He doesn't know how much I've tried. "Your skin's burning," I inform him. "You're way too fair-skinned to be outside without sunblock."

"Yeah." Silas opens his car door. "I'll be on my way. I'm going to look for something else to paint. Come by in the next couple days if you want to go to the darkroom, okay?"

"Okay," I say.

A squirrel pops up by the trash cans and picks up a piece of food, then runs away, reminding me of Myra saying I might have photoshopped that animal. If only

I could find that ferret. And then I get an idea. "Wait, Silas."

He pauses.

"What if you could paint a different place than this park *and* help me at the same time?" I ask.

CHAPTER
30

We drive over to the administration building. Someone's coming back inside, so we enter with him. There's one person who knows everyone in this town, the one person who's been here longer than anyone else.

Herb.

If anyone can get us authorization, Herb can. Herb's playing solitaire and drinking coffee from a large mug that says *World's Best Boss*. "Hi," I say, and he jumps.

"Tuesday!" He blinks at me as if I'm a ghost. "To what do I owe the honor? Library?"

I point at Silas. "This is the artist-in-residence. He needs your help." I know these are the right words to say. The artist-in-residence is a special thing. They usually only have two per year, so everyone wants to help them out. I explain how we need permission to get into Hedges.

Herb sighs and looks out the window. The sun makes a reflection in his glasses, so I can't see his eyes. "It doesn't seem like my place to get involved, Tuesday."

Silas leans forward. "I just want to get in there to paint."

"If you want to do it, then everyone will want to do it." Herb sputters through his nose, like some kind of horse.

My phone auto-connects with the Wi-Fi and pings with notifications. I've got a ton of notifications. Likes, comments . . . followers. Wait, what? "Silas! I have over two thousand followers!"

"I'm jealous," Silas says. "It took me years to get to a thousand."

"Kids always know tech better," Herb says.

"That's because for a long time you had too many photos of your tofu, Silas." I scroll down. The accounts more or less seem to be real people, not those bot accounts that follow everyone.

"You looked at my Instagram?" Silas says.

"Of course." I wonder why he thinks we wouldn't look at his social media.

"Everyone's looked at your Instagram," Herb says. "You're the artist-in-residence. What else is there to do around here?"

"Oh, I don't know." Silas points out the window at the mountains. "Look at majestic beauty? But I'd love to see some real pristine stuff. Like at Hedges."

Silas and I smile at Herb like he's our grandpa or something.

"Fine." Herb purses his lips. "I'll see what I can do."

Herb makes the call. I post the photo I took that has the prairie dog in it. *What animal do you think this is?* I ask on the post, then put a bunch of hashtags on it. I blow out a sigh of frustration. "When we go there, I want to look one more time for any sign of the ferret." I tell Silas what happened.

"I love mysteries," Silas says.

"Okay." Herb gets off the phone. "One catch. Old Herb's going to have go to with you."

"You?" I don't know if this is such a good idea.

"Me. Which means"—Herb pulls out his car keys— "I'm driving."

I try to ask Dana for permission first, I really do, but she's out in the field and can't answer. Instead I send her a text that she'll get as soon as she has a signal. *I AM GOING INTO HEDGES WITH HERB AND SILAS. IT IS 100% AUTHORIZED. THANK YOU.*

We drive into Hedges. The bouldering place says *Closed Until Further Notice.* I wonder what Carter's going to do with his time now, or if he even knows about this. Hopefully it'll reopen sooner rather than later.

We drive until the road ends at a bunch of construction

equipment, circled up like horses in a corral.

My stomach twists. Am I going to be able to find the ferrets? What if I was wrong and there was never even a prairie dog? Maybe it was all my wishful thinking after all.

Silas turns in his seat. "You lead us back to where you think they are, Tuesday. I'll help as much as I can."

I nod.

Silas gets out of the car. "I think what I'd like to do is take photos with my phone, then paint later."

"Let me show you the meadow I was talking about." I begin moving.

"What, like this meadow?" Herb gestures at where we are.

"No." I point upward. "There."

"Hmph," Herb says. "Why can't you take photos from down here?"

"You can wait in the car if you want, Herb," Silas tells him.

"Nope. I said I'd keep an eye on you, and that's what I'm going to do. What if you get bit by a rattler? Dana would never forgive me." Herb shuffles along.

We keep going for a while, walking quietly except for Herb's huffing and puffing. "Wait!" Silas keeps saying, and we pause to let him photograph what he wants.

"How far back do you want to go?" Herb leans on a

rock, red-faced. I hope he won't have a heart attack.

"We just have to go into the slot canyon and up a ridge," I say.

"Huh." Herb looks up at the canyon walls doubtfully.

Finally, we arrive at the meadow, and today it's even less clear where we saw the poop than it was the last time I came here with Myra. Everywhere I turn, the fallen trees look the same. I don't remember what was beyond them.

"Hey." Silas stops me. "You said you took photos here when you were with Carter, right?"

"Five," I say.

"Did you make the contact sheets?"

I nod and pull them out of my bag.

There are two images per sheet. "Are they in the order you took them?"

"Of course," I say. "I numbered them. That's how you're supposed to do it." I point to where I wrote in Sharpie. *1, 2, 3, 4, 5.*

"And when did you see the poop?"

I think back, looking at the photos. "Before five. But I'm not sure if it was before four or after."

"Okay." Silas holds up *4*. A tree branch with a boulder behind it. "Let's try retracing your steps using the photos."

I move to the edge, where Carter and I looked down

at the construction equipment. "Okay. This was the last one." I turn, my body remembering. I point. "We were over there."

I step away, then scan the landscape for the branches. He turns in a circle. "Look for a branch that has this right angle."

"Right there"—Herb points—"but from the other side."

We walk around the branch until we get to the correct angle. Then we look at the proof sheet again. "That's it," Silas agrees.

"And the boulder was the third." Now that we're in the exact right spot, it's easier to remember where I was.

I retrace my steps until I see the boulder. Yes, this is familiar now. That small, squat bush right in front of me. The canyon wall behind.

And then . . . I find poop. With more fresh poop near it. "Here!" I shout. I've never been so glad to see scat before.

CHAPTER

31

Herb and Silas rush over, and we all spend a few minutes exclaiming about how weird the poop looks. "I bet they mark their turf," Herb says. "That's what animals do."

"Why do you know about animals?" I ask.

"My dad used to take me hunting when I was a boy in Pennsylvania. That's how we got most of our food for the winter. Deer and pheasant."

Silas takes off his hat and looks around, then walks off. "Hey." He gestures. "Come look at this."

I go over to him. There are several mounds with holes at the top.

"Those look like prairie dog burrows," says Herb.

"Another thing you learned from boyhood?" Silas asks.

"No. I learned that at the zoo. They have a display

there, and that's what their burrows look like." Herb takes off his hat and mops his bald head. "Now let's mark where this thing is so we can show Myra."

One of the burrows is flattened, though, because the hole caved in. "Someone stomped it." Herb straightens with a huge frown.

Stomped it? "How can you tell?"

He points. There's a faint imprint of a boot in the dry dirt.

"Maybe they thought it was a snake hole." Silas squats to examine it.

"Even if it were a snake hole, they should have left it alone. Rattlesnakes have their place in nature. And this is nature."

"If they thought it was a rattlesnake hole, I can see why they'd do that. Nobody wants to get bitten while they're working." Silas sounds doubtful, though. "But they're working in the wilderness. Don't they expect that?"

"People always want things to be comfortable for them." Herb's voice is almost a growl. "And when this place is built into homes, the people who buy them will complain if there's a snake or a coyote in their backyards."

"It wasn't a snake, though. That's the point," I say.

"We'll get Myra out here to look." Herb takes a wire

that has a yellow flag attached to it out of his backpack and sticks it into the ground. "Now we can tell where it was. And I'll tell the supervisor that they're not to stomp it."

Herb and I start walking away, but Silas stays where he is, looking up. "Earth to Silas," Herb says in his grumbly way. "You want a ride home or not?"

"Sorry." Silas finally tears his eyes away from above. The sky is a brilliant cobalt blue above the canyon, shot through with pure white clouds. "Where the sky lives," he says, repeating the line from my uncle's poem. "It's close enough to touch here."

"It's not like that in California?" I ask.

"No. The sky is different wherever you go. We're higher up here. I live near the sea." Silas begins walking back with us. "The light is different, too. That's why I go all over the place to paint."

I consider this. I guess it's something I've noticed but not paid attention to, except when it had to do with the night sky. Also I haven't been that many places. We're from Nevada, so that's that.

When Herb gets back, he calls his friend while Silas and I get sodas out of the vending machine. "Cheers." Silas holds up his diet drink. "Job well done."

"You did a lot of it."

"But if you hadn't taken the photos, it would all have been lost," Silas says.

Herb lunges out of his office, red-faced. That can't be good. "What happened?" Silas asks.

"I told them they should stop construction until we can determine for sure whether those ferrets are there. And you know what they said? They said I'm just the fees man and I don't know anything." Herb's hammy hands clench into fists. "I am not going to take this lying down." He takes out his phone.

"Who are you calling?" I ask. I think if there's one way to make Herb mad, it's to tell him he's not important. I mean, that's pretty much a way to make anyone in the world mad, honestly.

"You don't get to be as old as me without knowing who's who around here. I'm calling my buddy Mark at the newspaper in Salt Lake. He'll be interested in this story."

"I'll repost your story, too," Silas says, "to my dozen followers."

"You've got more than that." I post the poop photos to my Instagram and type out a long story about it. *And now they won't stop doing construction even though they don't know whether or not these are ferrets.* Then I post. And wait.

CHAPTER

32

When Silas and I leave the administration building, I see Dana's car in the lot. "I'm going to see my mother," I tell him.

"Later, gator." Silas walks toward his car.

"Wait." He's only here for a few more days. "If I don't see you again before you leave . . ."

"You will." He gives me a half smile.

"I will?"

"Definitely for sure." He waves. "Good luck with the biologist."

Dana's in her office when I run in and tell her everything that happened today. "Slow down," she says. "Does Myra know?"

"Herb emailed her."

"Great. I'm sure she'll love Herb telling her how to do her job," Dana says dryly. She turns back to her computer.

"I don't want you to get your hopes up, Tuesday."

I sit on Dana's ball and bounce up and down. "My hopes," I say, "are at a perfectly reasonable level."

"What level is that?"

"Medium. Both Herb and Silas agree there's an animal living there."

"Still," Dana says.

I bounce up and down by the bookcase with the photo of Dana and Ezra from when they were kids, standing in the field with their cat. The one in my dream, black with a white spot on its chest and little white feet.

Little white feet like socks.

Like in my dream. I stop bouncing. "Dana," I say slowly. "What was your cat's name?"

"Socks. Because of his paws." Dana sounds absent. "Why?"

An electric thrill goes over me. My subconscious did the work for me! I almost fly off the ball. "Dana. Dana. This is what Ezra was talking about."

"What do you mean?"

"White socks in a field. You two camping. The poem."

Dana's fingers stop typing. "Hmmm." She turns and looks at me. "That could be right, but what does that have to do with anything? Why would he put that in a poem?"

I raise my right index finger. "One, Ezra was not

the type of person to randomly type up a riddle with no answer, for no reason at all. He created riddles for both of us."

"True," Dana says.

"Two, Ezra was very detail-oriented. If he wanted it to be easy, I believe he would have told you where to leave his ashes in that regular will he'd made."

Dana tilts her head to the side, nods. "I'll grant you that."

"So." I clear my throat. "Where did this camping take place?"

"On a mesa, kind of hidden away in the mountains. But that spot doesn't even exist anymore." She turns down her mouth. "There's a resort there now."

Interesting, and not surprising. "He must've meant somewhere around here. I mean, the second stanza says *Beyond the owl's pinions*. And I don't think Ezra would send us somewhere far away, not when he loved this place so much."

"I'm not sure it matters," Dana says. "Since we're moving."

I stop bouncing. "But you don't have the offer letter yet."

"I do." Dana brings up a file on her screen. "I got it this morning."

I look. There it is, in black and white. It has a start

date and everything. August 31. I also notice her salary is better than it is here.

I clear my throat. "Have you told everyone about the new job?"

"Not yet. I have to sign it." Dana closes her eyes. "I have twenty-four hours."

"Oh." I'm afraid to ask her if this means she might change her mind. Maybe it's not as final as I thought. Until we're driving out of Zion for the last time, there's a possibility things could change. Right?

But for now, I want her to figure out Ezra's last wishes with me. I swallow. "That's only a little more than a month. We could figure out the poem before we leave."

I bounce some more, trying to think of what I can say that'll convince her. I mean, I think we can—if only she would help me. But Dana has her own version of what's going on and that's what she wants to believe, no matter what.

I think of Silas and how angry he was that his ex moved on. But I don't know the ex's side. Similarly, Dana's not paying attention to my side—just hers.

Maybe we're all caught up in our own stories, and we don't even know it.

"Here's the thing." Dana finally turns to me. "I don't know if I want to leave him somewhere where I'm not going to be."

I'm so surprised she shared this with me that I can't think of anything to say. If she wants to spread the ashes where we live, though, then there might never be a permanent place that we'll never ever leave. Which means the ashes will stay in the urn, on whatever mantel we have, forever. I want to tell her he's already gone—does it really matter where his ashes are?

Dana's phone buzzes. "Myra's in Hedges and says to come meet her. Let's go."

"All right." I'll tell her later. Maybe.

It's pretty easy to spot Myra's car—an SUV covered in bumper stickers—but harder to find Myra. "She said to go straight south from her car until we see her," Dana says.

Finally we spot Myra, a few dozen feet off the trail, putting a tag on a lamb whose mother stands nearby. The lamb baas nervously, but it only takes a second for the tag, and Myra lets it go.

"What are you doing with the Hedges sheep?" Dana asks.

"These are bighorn hybrids." Myra pets the lamb. It does look different than the other lambs, its fur rougher, a little stockier. "What happens is that the male bighorns roam around and, well, this happens."

"Can't you move all the sheep out of here?" I ask.

"Not while it's privately owned. We're working on solutions."

A lot of things are always "we're working on it" in government. Myra picks up her gear and hands me a second backpack full of equipment. I almost fall over. "Ready to show me this thing?" Myra asks, and I nod.

I'm glad that Herb planted the flag—it makes it much easier to spot where it is from a distance. Myra examines the area. "This looks like prairie dog habitat."

"So not ferrets?" Dana says.

"Ferrets use the burrows of prairie dogs. It's very efficient—eat their prey, take their home." Myra takes a plastic bag out and scoops poop into it. "This doesn't look like the scat of gophers or prairie dogs." She gives me a serious look. "I think you could be right, Tuesday."

This doesn't make me feel as good as I thought, probably because Myra initially believed I was making this up. I nod and cross my arms, not meeting Myra's gaze.

"Tuesday! Please control your happiness." Dana gives a little laugh.

Myra smiles ruefully. "I know what it is. Tuesday, I'm sorry I thought you might have photoshopped the prairie dog. I should have known you wouldn't do something like that."

"Wait a sec." Dana frowns. "You thought Tuesday was lying?"

"She couldn't find the scat again or prove anything to me. It happens. I mean, we've both seen people scratch pictures into the sandstone and then pretend it's a new archaeological discovery." Myra cocks her head. "I'm sorry. I thought Tuesday would've told you about it."

"No. She didn't." Dana's voice is soft.

"I was going to, but then you told me about the whole job thing." I glare at my mother. "I was mad, so no. I did not tell you."

Dana turns a mottled pink. Myra turns away. "I'm going to set up a camera so we can record the burrow overnight."

I wish Myra hadn't brought that up at all. I'd rather watch her set up a camera than have this ultra-awkward moment with my mother. I walk toward the trail. "I'll go wait in the car."

"Hold on." Dana follows. "Tuesday. We need to talk."

"Later." I don't stop moving. I'm tired of Dana not hearing me, of always having to be careful of what I bring up with her but not the other way around.

"I don't want you to think you can't come to me."

I stop and turn around to face her. Her face is still red. "You know, for someone who tells me to think about feelings, you don't seem to think of mine very much."

"That's not true."

I put my hands on my hips. "Then help me solve Uncle Ezra's riddle once and for all. Together."

She stares at me, and I stare back. Then she looks at the ground, a single tear falling out of her eye. "I can't," she says quietly.

"Why not? Because you want to take his ashes with you everywhere? You know he wouldn't want that."

"Because"—she sniffles—"because if we do this last thing . . ."

She trails off. The breeze comes and lifts her hair off her head. I wait, watching my mother. Her expressionless mask seems to fall off, and her face droops with sadness and confusion. Which is odd, because I didn't think Dana Beals was ever confused about anything.

It suddenly occurs to me that my mother is a totally separate person from me, who has thoughts I will never know, and it feels strange. Sort of like when you see a teacher outside the classroom and you're surprised, because you never thought of them living outside the room where you see them, though you know in your head that doesn't make sense. It's still how you feel.

Dana meets my eyes. "If we do this last thing with his ashes, it'll mean he's really gone." She pauses again and swallows audibly. "And I don't want him to be."

She faces me, her arms slightly lifted at her sides, her fingers clenched. I remember what Silas said about how Dana hadn't mourned Ezra, hadn't truly said goodbye. Maybe this is part of it.

It seems like she needs a hug, but that's not my thing.

When I was young, in preschool—which is as far back as I remember—Dana would ask me for permission to hug me. And when I was around four, I started saying no. I didn't like the feeling, always too warm and too tight, though I'm sure she wasn't squeezing me. I didn't like smelling her deodorant, which made my nose itchy, or feeling the texture of her shirt against my arms. I couldn't breathe, and I wanted to push her off.

"Do you want a hug?" I ask her now, because I think that's a thing I should do.

Dana smiles at me, and somehow she erases all the emotions from her face again. From below, the rumbly low roar of construction equipment starts up again. The hands unclench and stretch. "I don't know about you, but I could use an ice-cream cone."

Dana holds out her arms, and I step into them. For a moment, I'm reminded of the last time I hugged Uncle Ezra. Then the moment is gone, and it's Dana. I step back. "Okay. I'm ready for us to eat our feelings."

CHAPTER
33

We sit on a bench outside the ice-cream parlor/deli/ tourist shop where we get our cones. It's the height of tourist season, so their very small parking lot was full, and we had to park several long blocks away near the library, at a paid lot.

I'm having mint chip, and Dana's having caramel pecan. We have to eat kind of fast, because the sun's melting the ice cream all over our hands, dripping onto the sidewalk. The concrete is covered in splatters of different colors, green and pink and white, like a painting. A gross, dirt covered painting, but still a painting.

That reminds me. "Silas is leaving the day after tomorrow," I say to Dana.

"That's right. End of June." She nods. "He's been so nice to you. Do you want to get him a thank-you gift?"

"I think he was nice to me because he wanted to be, not to get anything." I wipe my mouth with the extra napkins I took and hand another one to her. She always forgets those.

She takes it with a smile. "I know. It would be a thoughtful thing to do."

So we go into the gift store. I'm not at all sure Silas would want any of these T-shirts that say *Zion National Park* or bags of polished rocks. Or a keychain with his name on it—though they don't have his anyway.

Then I get to a tall glass display filled with small ceramic animal figures. They have a bunch of different ones—most of which don't live here, like tigers and elephants and pandas.

Stuck in the back behind a giraffe is a miniature ceramic ferret.

"This," I announce.

We return to the car, the ferret wrapped in tissue paper. "I've been thinking," Dana says. "You might be right about Ezra and the poem being a riddle."

"I know I'm right."

She laughs. "I have to say, I hope you're always this confident, Tuesday."

My face gets hot—hotter than it already was from the sun. "Well, I'm only this confident when I have enough evidence. And I believe that I do." I look at her carefully. "Are you ready?"

"Almost. Very nearly." My mother nods. "Yes. I think so."

We pass the little free library, and both of us stop, as we always do, to see if there's anything new inside. I open it up and take out a few titles.

Dana wrinkles her nose. "Nothing's calling out to me. *How to Get Over your Codependent Relationship?*"

"Huh." I pull that out. It's a workbook, completely empty. On the back it says, *Are you having trouble putting your past behind you?*

I tuck it under my arm. "I'm going to hang on to this. In case."

CHAPTER

34

Myra told me I could come to work with Dana so I can look at what the camera captured. The first thing in the morning, we pick up Carter and drive to the offices.

Every office in the science bungalow is empty. "Hello?" Dana says, and nobody answers. Voices murmur from the far end. Myra's office. Carter and I run the rest of the way.

All the interns crowd around Myra's monitor, five people deep. Carter and I push our way in. Myra looks at me with shining eyes. "Hey! Come look. Let me rewind."

The crowd parts, and we make our way forward. The monitor shows a black-and-white scene—the night vision of the camera. I recognize the burrow area, and the short scrubby bush next to it.

A furry little head pops out, its nose sniffing and its whiskers twitching. It looks mostly light-colored with a black face. After examining the ground for a while, it puts its forelegs on the edge and hoists its long body out, then scurries away.

Suddenly I'm covered in goosebumps. I can hardly believe what I'm seeing.

Carter gasps. "That's no gopher."

"It is indeed a black-footed ferret," Myra says.

The interns murmur. *Wow. Amazing.*

Dana puts her arm around me. "You were right, Tuesday."

I nod, my body sagging with relief. I know this won't necessarily make a huge difference in the numbers of the overall development—maybe ten houses—but it does mean they won't be able to build up there at all. One more section that will stay pristine. We watch it again and again as if we're watching the first moon landing, all full of wonder. Maybe outsiders would question why we care about a weasel so much, but to us it's important. Carter records it on his phone.

"Good job," someone says, and I look up. It's Nick.

"Thanks." I find my eyes are wet for some reason. I wipe them with the back of my hand. Dana draws me closer to her, and this time, instead of pulling away like I usually would, I lean in.

Work gets halted temporarily after Myra calls the state offices and tells them what's going on. Now the state's sending out its own wildlife biologist who deals with this kind of thing. In the meantime, Myra will monitor the camera's feed. The black-footed ferrets are nocturnal, she explained, so during the daytime there won't be much going on.

"I thought shutting it down would take longer," I say to Dana, because she's always complaining about how much time bureaucracies take, and unnecessary red tape, and things like that.

"They have procedures in place to protect animals and other resources," she says. "Nobody wants to dig through an endangered animal's nest."

I put the clip of the ferret on my Instagram. One of my followers starts a petition. *Sign this to stop the development at Zion!* it says. Within a few hours, it has a couple thousand signatures. However, it's not like if they get to a certain number, the developer would automatically *do* anything. But it makes me feel hopeful. People are paying attention.

This is just the first step—telling as many people as possible about the problem and getting them to care. Now the state biologist has to come, and Dana says some judge will decide what to do next. If a lot of people tell the state they don't want the development, it might shut it down.

Then, the next day, news reporters start showing up. There are three vans in the office parking lot with satellite dishes sticking out from the top, plus a couple more people in regular cars, who work for newspapers.

"Finally." Herb peers out the window. He's in his park uniform, his hair carefully combed and his face freshly shaven instead of whiskery. He's nervous.

"Is all this because of your friend at the paper?" I ask.

"The news was interested." Herb nods with satisfaction. "Now everybody in Utah's going to know about the ferret. We'll have protestors swarming the area within days."

I don't know if I like the sound of more people showing up. "If it'll help . . . but the state's sending a biologist."

Herb makes a dismissive sputtering noise with his lips. "State! I don't trust them any further than I could throw them."

Before I can respond, Dana shows up with a reporter in tow. "Tuesday, this reporter would like to interview you for the local news."

"Sure."

Dana leans down next to my ear. "Don't be nervous."

It hadn't occurred to be me to be nervous before she said that. Now sweat pools under my arms. "Um. Okay." I have to get this right.

A sound person clips a microphone onto my T-shirt. "Do you have a pocket to put this in?" She hands me the box the wire's attached to.

I slip this into my back pocket. My hand shakes a little. I remind myself that I'm not going to be pushed off a cliff or anything. The worst thing that can happen is I stutter.

The woman who's interviewing me comes into my mom's office. She smiles. She looks shiny, as if someone sprayed a coat of shellac over her makeup, and not a single hair is out of place. It probably took this lady like three hours to get ready, which makes me instantly decide that being on TV is not for me, generally speaking. "I'm Shelby Jones, reporter at large." She holds out her hand.

"Tuesday."

"Nice to meet you." She points at the camera some man is holding. "When that red light comes on, we'll be live. You look at me, not at the camera, like we're having a little old conversation. Okay? Not a thing to worry about."

I square my shoulders. "I'm not worried."

"She's got nerves of steel," the sound lady says, and picks up a pole that has a mic dangling off the end of it.

I think about how scared I am of heights. "I'd say that's a bit of an exaggeration." But no one is listening, and soon the reporter lady is pointing that mic at me.

"So. We're live with Tuesday Beals and Myra Evans, the wildlife biologist who discovered the ferrets. Tuesday, how do you feel about your discovery?"

"Good," I say.

"It's amazing," Myra says. "I never expected to find black-footed ferrets here."

"And here's the little girl who could," Shelby says. "You certainly are smart, aren't you?" She sounds the way adults sound when they want to pat me on the head.

I frown.

"She's very bright," Myra says. "More importantly, perhaps, she doesn't give up."

Shelby blinks at Myra as if she doesn't quite get that. "Right. She didn't give up." She smiles at Myra. "However, here's a question for you. What would you tell people who don't have affordable housing? Because the Hedges development would solve some of the housing crisis in the area." I look at Myra in alarm, but she's staring at the woman, frozen.

I speak up. "I mean, they could build houses on land that's not right next to a national park. There's lots of other open space in this state."

"And . . . that's not what this is about," Myra says. "This is about the ferret and saving the habitat of an endangered species."

"But you stopped the whole project," the woman says. "When you simply could fence off the area where the ferrets are."

"It's only stopped *temporarily*. It could restart after we do a little investigating," Myra says in what I think is a very reasonable tone. "If they're in that area, they could be in other places."

I'm huffing a little bit. Shelby opens her mouth, but I speak first. "Allow me to explain." I'm not supposed to look into the camera, but I don't care, so I do. I want to say this to everybody watching. Not to Shelby the reporter.

I stand up as straight as I can and look into the gaping black hole of the camera lens. I pretend Ezra is on the other side of it, nodding, and this gives me the little push of courage I need. "There are thousands of pristine or near-pristine acres of land on Hedges. *Pristine* means they haven't been touched. The other acreage has been developed by indigenous tribes such as the Paiute, and, later, Mormon settlers—which I don't even want to get into."

The woman's smile fades.

"This land is more pristine than Zion, actually. Nobody's out there parking all over the vegetation or scaring away animals. And if this land got developed, Zion would no longer qualify as a Dark Sky area. Which means the sky at night would be light-polluted.

"Even though this area isn't part of the park, it's right next to it." I inhale, remembering the Merchant Mario's lady. "Imagine that you suddenly got a next-door neighbor who made a lot of noise, partied all night, and had lights shining on your house. It would change your life, wouldn't it?"

"I'm not sure I'm following," says the reporter.

"Zion would be changed if the land right next to it got built up. And the big new houses aren't going to be very affordable for the people who need housing the most. So what's more important?" I squint. "That people get their Merchant Mario's, or the preservation of a natural resource?"

"I think there's a balance," the woman says.

"There's not, as far as I'm concerned." I'm not sure where all these words are coming from. It's like I've been thinking them all along—picking them up from my reading, from talking to Myra and Dana and everyone else who always discusses these things—and they've suddenly come together. "People need to wake up and do the right thing. There are other cities to live in."

The woman turns to the camera. "And thank you to Tuesday Beals for that. Wow."

The sound person unclips the microphone, and I thread it out from my shirt. "That was great," she says in a low voice.

I shrug. "I'm just telling the truth."

After the interview, I need fresh air. I feel exposed, somehow—the same as when Nick made a comment about me being smart. I tell myself it doesn't matter. I go into the parking lot—which is the only exit from the building—and stand in the sunshine. It feels good to inhale non-air-conditioned oxygen.

A van crawls into the lot. Another news station? I didn't think there were that many. No, it's a camping van, one I haven't seen before. Probably an out-of-place tourist. I prepare myself to tell them where the campground is.

The van parks, and a man with dark skin and curls gets out and starts walking toward me. He's wearing a salmon-pink T-shirt, stained with sweat, a pair of frayed shorts, and flip-flops. "Hello! I'm the state wildlife biologist. Is this the building entrance?"

"Yes!" The state wildlife biologist. That's good news. "You must be here to see Myra."

He smiles widely at me. "I'm Reggie Haskins."

"Tuesday Beals."

He points at me. "The one with the Instagram, right? That was good work you did. Myra told me all about it." He holds out his fist.

I stare at it for a few seconds. Oh, right. "Bump," I say, and bump his fist. No matter how many times Carter does that to me, it's still not something I expect other people to do.

I help Reggie get into the building. Knowing that he'll be watching over the ferrets makes me feel instantly better. As if someone, somewhere, is listening and cares. For the first time in a month, maybe longer, a weight gets lifted off me. I hadn't even realized I was so worried. I almost skip home, my steps finally light.

CHAPTER

35

L ater that evening, I'm at Carter's house. We're working on a Lego robot, a kit that Carter got a while
back, and eating pizza that Grant made.

I look at the directions and snap on a single square
piece. The kit's half done. I hope we can finish it before I
move. Us moving to another state seems so unreal, like
talking about me going to college one day—part of me
doesn't want to believe it.

"So what do you think will happen now with the
development?"

I grit my teeth. "The state wildlife biologist will figure out where the ferrets are living. The developer won't
be able to build there. But Myra doesn't think they're
spread out very far—just in that one area that's like the
plains." I concentrate, considering how many random
spots the ferrets must be in between here and Bryce
Canyon, where they probably originated. How many

things like this do we accidentally overlook?

It *is* like looking for the comets in the night sky. You have to be lucky sometimes and be in the right place at the right time.

"So what are they going to do, fence off the ferret area?" Carter squints at the directions, then changes a piece he just placed.

"I don't know. Reggie's going to do a survey, and then he says he's going to sit there and make sure the construction people don't disturb them." That's Reggie's job—he has to go all over the state protecting animals. He camps out in his van, watching to make sure nothing happens at the sites.

I look at Carter. He doesn't know about Dana's job yet, unless Dana told his parents. I doubt she did, though. He would've mentioned it.

"Carter," I say. "What would you do if one of us moved?"

I expect him to laugh me off, but he has an unusual reaction. His shoulders hunch, and he gives me a strange look. "What—what are you talking about?"

Maybe he does know. "Um. People here. They move all the time. Right?"

"Everyone except Herb."

I inhale a breath, but there's a knock on the door, and both of us leap up to answer it. It's Silas and Danielle, and Silas has a box of Girl Scout cookies. Thin Mints.

He's referencing the first day we came over, when he asked if we were selling cookies. I laugh and open the door and go outside.

He shakes the box at us.

"Where did you get those?" I ask.

"I have my ways," he says.

"The way is through my freezer," Danielle says. "I always buy extras. They keep very well."

He hands me the box. "Thought I'd stop and say goodbye."

I'd almost forgotten. I'd planned on stopping by with his going-away gift. "You're leaving tomorrow, right?"

He nods. "Early, though. I have a long drive."

Danielle claps her hands. "We saw the interview! What a wonderful job you did."

"Ugh." I want to forget about it forever. "I gave a whole lecture."

"I thought it was awesome." Carter sits on the step. "I put it on Instagram and tagged you."

"What?" I don't want any extra people to watch it. I don't need people to know who I am. "Why?"

"Because it was great," Carter says simply.

We open the box and parcel out the cookies.

"The reporter was asking hard questions," Silas says. "To a kid!"

"I think she was asking Myra," I say.

"The reporter's gotten a ton of backlash," Silas says.

"And, of course, people around here don't want any-thing to happen to the ferret," Danielle says.

"Maybe they should leave the whole ranch alone and charge people a fee to do things like hike and take pho-tos," Silas says.

"Maybe, but that would limit access." Danielle shakes her head. "I used to teach art in schools around here—and there are always a bunch of kids who have never been inside Zion, even though it's right here. They can't afford the fee."

I actually did know about that. In fourth grade, you get a national parks pass, and here they do a field trip into Zion. Still, I'd kind of taken it for granted that I'm allowed to do all this stuff inside the park while so many people never have that opportunity.

My phone buzzes. I look at my Instagram notifica-tions and gasp. I'm on a celebrity gossip account that chooses me as "The GOAT of the Day." *Look at this little girl own this woman*, it says. "I'm not a celebrity."

"*GOAT* means 'greatest of all time,'" Carter says from beside me. "It's a compliment!"

I scowl at the phone again. GOAT? "How can I be the 'greatest of all time' of the *day*? There should be one for all of time. This makes no sense. I'm going to write to them to take my name off."

"I know it doesn't make sense, but it's the internet," Carter says, as if that justifies anything. It is, however, a good explanation, which is different than an excuse.

Carter yelps. "Hey! Lyla Redding liked your photo again! And look what she wrote."

"Follow this Tuesday kid," I read aloud. *"She knows what's up. Write to your Senator and tell them to #Keep-ZionDark!"* New likes and comments are coming in as we hold the phone.

"Good job, kiddo! You're moving the needle!" Silas says.

I turn off the notifications. Maybe so, but I don't want to think about Instagram right now. I want to be here with Carter and Silas and Danielle. I stick a cookie in my mouth and smile at them.

We sit on the stoop, each of us munching our cookies and thinking whatever separate thoughts we have. It's nice to be with people who don't have to talk all the time. The wind blows through the oak tree that overhangs the yard and the breeze hits my face and blows my hair back. I look up at the tree, noticing the shape of the leaves and the negative space where you can see bits of sky. I've never looked at the leaves like that before. Maybe I'll take a photo later.

Taking photos isn't just fun—it's changed me. It seems to me that this past month I've been seeing things differently. Observing details I'd never noticed before. It's because when you set up for a photo—a photo that is going to be on a negative that costs money—you have to be as sure as you can that your shot is right. Now my brain is getting trained to look at everything as if it's a potential photo.

I run to get them my gifts for Silas. There was no time to wrap. Silas looks up at me as I jump off the stoop and land in front of him. "Here." I thrust them at him.

"What's this?"

"Just some appreciation." I shrug, then eye Carter, who's looking a little embarrassed that he didn't bring anything. "It's from Carter, too."

"Wait. I want to see what you gave him before you say it's from me, too." I think Carter is joking.

Silas takes the tissue off the ferret. "Oh! Our little friend." He clutches the figure to his chest. "I will always remember this time in Zion, Tuesday. Thank you."

"That's also from me," Carter says.

I nod, pleased. And then he looks at the book I handed him. *"How to Get Over your Codependent Relationship,"* he reads, and guffaws his Silas guffaw. "Perfect!"

Carter clears his throat. "That, however, is most definitely not from me."

Silas laughs again, then looks at me, Carter, and Danielle. "Seriously, though." His eyes well up. "You all have helped me more than you could ever know. I was a mess when I got here. Now . . ." He closes his eyes, tilts his head back.

"You've been reborn?" Danielle says.

Silas laughs. "I don't know about reborn. But I've been able to let go of a lot of things. Accept stuff." He shakes his head. "And kind of understand my part in all of it, too."

"Yes. Until you work through something, you're going to keep hitting your head on that wall and never move forward." Danielle pops another Thin Mint into her mouth. "A good lesson for anyone."

I think about this, and how Dana doesn't seem to understand it. But things have been a bit better since the day we found the ferrets. "Is there any way to get someone to understand that quicker?"

"People don't change unless they're ready," Danielle answers.

This is not an acceptable answer for me. Unlike Silas and his husband, I can't end my relationship with Dana—nor do I want to. And I can't imagine having Ezra's urn in the house forever, that part of the story always unfinished.

Silas stands up. "I have to finish packing. Thank you for everything."

Carter throws his arms around Silas in a bear hug. "Thanks for helping us, Silas."

"Yeah, thanks," I say. I offer my hand.

Silas shakes it. "Tuesday, you keep being you. The you-est you you can be."

I raise an eyebrow, unsure of what he means, exactly. "Okay."

"Don't be strangers to the studio, you two," Danielle says. "I'm always open to you." She looks me right in the eyes, and I know she means it.

I get flooded with emotions that I can't even name, like rising water inside me, so I just nod. "Thanks." My voice crackles.

They get in Danielle's car and drive off, Silas leaning out and waving the whole time. I wonder if I'll ever see him again. That's also how Dana and I sent off Ezra— standing here until his car disappeared from view. Carter and I do that now, waving until our arms ache and the car is gone and the only thing that remains is the red dust, still hanging in the air.

CHAPTER
36

When I get home from Carter's, Dana's sitting in the living room, the urn on the coffee table in front of her and the poem on her lap, a notebook beside her and a pen in her hand.

"Are you okay?" I step toward her.

She reads the poem out loud:

At the place beyond the meadows
On the table where we ate
In white socks we used to roam

Sitting still in darkness
Lit with the molecules of life
Beyond the owl's pinions

Where the sky lives

Is where I'm most at home

Please find it right away
To sleep there again
For a price I never wanted to pay

Dana lifts up the notebook. "I think you're right that the white socks refer to our cat, and to a place where we went camping."

I can't believe she's finally doing this. "But not the actual place from when you were kids, right?" I sit next to her, almost afraid to touch her and stop her thoughts.

"Right. White socks was a clue for me—about the cat. But he's definitely talking about that one place I mentioned, where you didn't want to go." She smiles at me. "It was this little mesa high up in Hedges. We saw an owl while we were hiking up there, back in a rock crevasse, just like you and Carter." Dana shakes her head. "It wasn't an easy place to get to. Especially if you've got a baby in your belly."

But of course Dana managed, because she's Dana. *"Lit with the molecules of life,"* I read aloud, and remember Ezra talking about how we're all made of stardust chemicals. "That's easy. He means a place that's good for star viewing." I lean toward her.

She nods. "It's the highest place in Hedges."

"But . . . can we get into Hedges to spread ashes?" That seems like the kind of thing they don't want us to do—it's not helping anyone but ourselves.

She shakes her head. "I'm not sure the developers will let us in for that reason, unless we lie about it. And that's wrong."

"Yeah." We gaze at the wooden box.

"We'll figure something out. I promise."

Ezra used to say that I could figure out any intellectual problem I wanted. "As long as you give it time to marinate, Tuesday, you'll be golden," he said. "Your mind will figure it out on its own if you give it space."

After all these months of not knowing what the poem meant, it all came together at once. And he was right. My brain remembered the cat and the camping. Dana remembered the rest. I needed my mother to complete the puzzle. Ezra had to know we'd only be able to solve it together. "What made you decide to look at this today?" I ask her.

She shrugs. "The ferrets."

"The ferrets?" I repeat. "How?"

"I mean, you finding the ferrets," Dana clarifies. "How you didn't give up. I wanted you to, honestly. I thought it was a hassle, all for nothing. But if you hadn't, we wouldn't have found them." She turns her head to smile at me. "You didn't give up on this, either. It made me think of how much I've been avoiding it." Dana sniffles. "Avoiding . . . dealing with my grief."

Both of us go quiet. I hear us breathing, low and deep, as if we're about to go to sleep.

And then I can feel Uncle Ezra in the room, as though he's standing behind us, solid and real but unseen. My breath catches. It's the same sensation I get when I make a new star discovery or when I created a photo. Like wonder and something else I can't describe.

Or maybe I can. Maybe it's love.

Dana grabs my hand with her cold one. Cold hands, warm heart, both Dana and Ezra always said, because it was a thing their parents said. Which makes no scientific sense because one is physical and the other emotional, but sometimes people say things that make them feel better, and that's okay. She's shuddering, her hair like a curtain over her face, and I realize she's crying.

I take my hand out of hers and put it on her back. "Dana?"

She turns to me, and the crying turns into sobbing, so deep it's as if it's coming from inside her belly. I grip her, and she cries onto my shoulder as if she's the child and I'm the mother for the moment.

I hold her the way she held me when I cried as a little kid—which was a lot, I was always upset about something—and stroke the back of her head. "Shh, shh, it's okay," I say, even though it's not okay, and it'll never be okay, at least, not in the same way it was before. But it'll still be okay. That doesn't make much sense, I know, but what does make sense is that everything is different, including us, and it's time to move forward. "It's okay," I say again, to let her know I'm here.

"I've got you," I tell my mother. "I've got you."

37

I go to work the next day with Dana and spend most of it in the library, looking at the ClearNights forum and catching up with everything there. Dana tells Julie she's going to leave, so now it's official. I don't think Julie immediately emails everyone, but it's not a secret anymore.

Dana shows me places we can rent in South Dakota— cute bungalows where I'll have my own bathroom. Not that I need that. "And internet, right?" I ask Dana.

"Of course we'll get internet," she says. "I promised."

It feels so good to believe her again.

In the evening, Carter, Grant, and Jenny pick me up. We go to a place that has my favorite burger, which is giant and comes with an egg on it, and shoestring fries that come in a paper cone that's set upright in a wire holder. I usually eat about half, which means I get lunch the next day. Grant, in his ranger uniform, gets a discount, as do all locals.

We've just ordered when the door opens and Reggie comes in. "I ordered food to go," he tells the host, then waves at us.

"Reggie!" I say. "How's it going?"

"Well," Reggie says. "They've restarted the construction."

"Already?" I squeak in surprise. "They're not even looking at the rest of the land?"

"Myra looked at some of it. But the construction people appealed the judge and got the first decision overturned." Reggie shakes his head. "Now they're only doing the barest minimum of what they're required to do within the law. So they can develop pretty much everything down below the ferret mesa."

My shoulders slump. I look at Carter. "That's like next to nothing."

"So, what? That mesa will be a protected wildlife area?" Grant asks.

"Looks like it's headed that way." The host hands Reggie his bag, and he takes it. "I mean, the only thing that can end construction at this point is pressure on the landowner, making it so they'll lose more money than they'd make. The almighty dollar." He opens the bag and eats a fry. "If you'll excuse me."

"Thanks for the update," I say.

Reggie nods. "No problem."

Carter and I slide down in the booth until our noses are the same height as the table. So finding the ferrets didn't do a whole lot of good at all. The news coverage only helped a little, apparently. "At least the mesa won't be built up," Carter says.

"Yeah." Uncle Ezra would be happy about that, at least. But with all that noise and activity, will the ferrets ever really have a shot at a comeback? A new depression sinks over me.

The food arrives. The burger smells awesome, but my stomach curls like I already ate too much at Thanksgiving. Not even Carter is hungry. We pick at our food.

"Don't be down, kids," Jenny says. "There's nothing you can do about it."

"You gave it your best shot," Grant agrees. He tries to change the subject and looks at Carter. "How was basketball yesterday?"

"It was cool." Carter sips his chocolate milkshake. He coughs—frozen drinks always make Carter cough.

"How about you, Tuesday? What's new with you and your mom?" Grant asks.

I wonder if he knows about Dana. "Why do you ask?"

"Because . . . you and Dana are our friends." Grant and Jenny exchange a look.

Oh no. On top of the news that Reggie just told us, now I have to tell them we're moving. If the superintendent talks about it first, it'll seem wrong that I didn't say anything. I take a deep breath. "I have to tell you something."

They wait.

"My mother got a job at South Dakota State University," I say, in one big rush. "We're moving." I shut my eyes so I don't have to see Carter's face. "I'm sorry."

"No! That's great!" Carter squeezes my arm.

My eyes snap open. "Great? You don't care that I'm leaving?"

"That's not it." Carter looks at his parents.

Jenny nods. "You can tell her if you want, sweetie."

Carter inhales and turns to me. "I have news, too."

He sounds so serious that I get scared. "Okay."

"My mom's having a baby."

I almost faint with relief. "Oh! That's fantastic! You've always wanted a brother or sister! I thought you were going to say something bad."

Carter looks down. "But we have to move."

"So you'll move into town to a bigger place," I say. "Babies are small. You don't have to worry about it for a while." I can't believe it. A baby! This is good news. Carter is always so nice to little kids. He'll be a great big brother.

But they all go still. Watching me. "Grant applied to transfer to the Great Smoky Mountains National Park, in North Carolina," Carter says. "We're moving, too."

Grant leans forward. "They need me there in three weeks."

I grip my milkshake glass, icy cold under my hand, and decide this must be another joke I don't get. "No, you're not." Even if I have to move myself, I can't imagine one of us not staying here. Who will I visit when I come back?

"Tuesday." Grant looks at me with his kind eyes. "You know park rangers tend to move around a lot."

"Well, they're about to build a bunch of new houses," I say. "Maybe you can get one." That might be a solution, I think. There aren't enough houses for everyone who wants to live here. But should so many people want to live here? My head hurts. "I don't want you to go."

"I know," Grant says.

"But now you don't have to feel bad for moving," Carter, Mr. Always-on-the-Bright-Side, says. "Because I'm moving, too! And now you don't have to worry about the ranch so much!"

I push away my fries. "I'm not going to stop worrying about the ranch just because we both move." I can't understand why he would say that. "The ranch is still going to be here. The development is still going to pollute the night sky."

"Yeah," Carter says, his voice fainter now. "It's bad. But at least we don't have to see it happen."

"That's not the point." I think about all the other

things we do that don't affect us. "It's better for the planet, not just for us. And for the people who are coming here after we leave."

"Tuesday's right," Grant says. "We have to be good stewards. We clean up after a picnic in the park so the next group won't have trouble. We're the only people who can make sure things keep going for years to come. We have to be good stewards."

Carter gets quiet. "I didn't think about it like that."

I still don't know how to process the fact that Carter is moving, too. In a few weeks, I might never see Carter again.

Jenny gets up to use the restroom, and I notice that her belly is sticking out a little bit, just enough that it looks like she had a big burrito or something. But instead, she's growing a human being.

Suddenly the concept that she is producing an actual human in there, made out of her flesh, is overwhelming. Like the first time I saw planets in detail and learned about them, and realized how short our lives are compared to how long the universe has been around.

I take one of Carter's tater tots. "We're definitely going to see each other again."

"Was it ever a question?" Carter says. "You'll visit me. I'll visit you." His phone buzzes, and he looks at it, then hits my arm excitedly. "Tuesday!" Carter shows me.

Lyla Redding has posted a photo of herself at Zion.

Heading back to Zion tomorrow! Follow #KeepZionDark for updates.

"Great." I shake my head. "All she's going to do is make the park more popular and crowded and do nothing to actually save it. How's that going to help?"

"I don't know," Carter admits. "I mean, maybe she'll have a protest or something."

"I hope not," Grant grumbles. "Those are difficult to manage."

Jenny returns, patting Grant's shoulder as she sits. "I'd love to see a protest if it helped out the park." She whips her head toward Grant. "Democracy is worth a little inconvenience, wouldn't you say?"

"Well. When you put it like that." He brushes off his fingers. "Let me reach out to her people and see exactly what she's planning on doing."

"Wait." I can't quite believe the words that are coming out of my mouth. "Can you ask them if Carter and I can meet with her?"

Carter squints at me. "What are you planning, Tuesday?"

I smile at him and shrug. "I don't know yet. I have to talk to Dana first. But maybe we can all figure it out together."

38

I n the morning, Grant drives us to the museum, where Lyla Redding is getting a tour of the history of the park from the museum assistant. Today Lyla's dressed in shorts, a plain white T-shirt, and running shoes. You wouldn't be able to tell she's a billionaire cosmetics company owner who's not even twenty-five yet.

"Tuesday!" Lyla holds out her hand for me to shake. "I remember you. The bird girl who posts about Hedges."

"You do? I wasn't sure that you actually saw the stuff on Instagram or if it was an assistant." I take my hand back.

"Well, she and I are practically the same person, so it probably doesn't matter," Lyla says.

"Hey, Lyla," Carter says. "I'm Carter. I don't think you ever got my name."

"Hey." She makes him blush just by waving at him. "Anyway, I'm so glad you've been posting about Hedges,

Tuesday. I would never have known about the history of the ranch or the ferrets." She points at an aerial view of Zion where you can see Hedges to the right. "I actually put a bid on it when it was for sale, but the developer outbid me."

"Were you going to build houses, too?"

She blinks. "No. Are they actually covering the whole thing with houses? I thought they were building like twelve estate homes on ten-acre lots. Just a few, all spread out, so it still looked like countryside."

"Not at all." I remember the plans from the meeting. "It's going to be houses from here," I point to the entrance, "back here and this way. Only this part, where there's an archaeological dig, will be spared. And this mesa, which is where we found the ferrets."

Lyla frowns. "Won't they at least make sure the lights on the houses all turn downward so the atmosphere isn't as affected?"

Oh. So she does know some stuff. "With the density of these houses, that's not going to work," Grant says. "If each house had some acreage, yeah, sure. But we're talking about each lot being only a few thousand square feet."

Lyla shakes her head. "Sounds like nobody's thinking of the overall future of this place."

"I know, right?" Carter says.

"I wasn't aware of the archaeological sites." Lyla

squints at the photo. "Are there many back there?"

"Quite a few." I figure now is the time to ask. I've already checked with Dana. "Would you like to see some archaeology?"

Grant drives us over in his Jeep. The wind blows Lyla's auburn hair back.

"Your hair smells like coconut!" Carter shouts at her.

"I'm sure she knows that, Carter," I say. "It's her shampoo."

"I was complimenting her," he says.

"Stating a fact isn't a compliment," I say. "The sky is blue is a fact. Saying the blue sky is pretty is a compliment. Why don't you tell her what you meant—that you find the smell of her hair enjoyable."

Carter turns bright red. "I think I'll sit here quietly instead."

Grant chuckles. Lyla laughs, the sound sweet.

Lyla tells us she grew up in California in a wine-making family that owns vineyards in Napa Valley. This seems to impress Grant, but it doesn't mean anything to Carter or me. She started her own lipstick line when she was a teenager. "I wanted something that was matte but didn't dry out my lips like most matte lipsticks."

I know from working with Danielle that "matte" means a flat finish, the opposite of "glossy," which means a shiny finish, but I'm not sure what she means in terms of lipstick.

"It means it's matte like paper, no shine at all, which means there's lack of moisture, right?" Carter says, surprising me.

"Exactly. So I added a special moisturizer." Lyla seems impressed, and he blushes in a pleased way.

We pull up to Hedges. Now there's a security guard sitting there at a podium under an umbrella. He has a little mister attached to the podium that sprays water in his direction. "We're with the park," Grant says, "going to see the archaeologist."

"Go ahead," the man barely glances at Grant's pass, probably because he's in his ranger uniform, and off we go.

We pass the new building that's going up and the roaring construction equipment. Lyla groans. "Ugh, that building's going to be a monstrosity! How can they tear apart the vegetation like that?"

"I know, right?" Carter says.

I'm hoping seeing all this stuff up front will get Lyla fired up enough to call the "Red-Pack Nation" into full action to protest Hedges. I'm not sure if it'll work, but having a couple million people against this development will probably bring it a lot more attention. Lyla can also get on to talk shows and national news and other things that I can't.

Dana and the students are working on the riverbank. Today they've put up a shade awning over their work area, so they're easy to spot as we drive up the road. Dana straightens as Delilah the Jeep pulls up and we get out.

"Hi there." Dana pulls off her work gloves. "I'm the cultural resource manager."

"That means archaeologist," I inform Lyla.

"Lyla Redding." Lyla shakes Dana's hand.

Cass the grad student squeals. "It's Lyla!" Then she and Na and Dante hurry past Dana to stand in front of Delilah.

People running up to me like that would make me feel awkward, but Lyla doesn't seem to mind. "Hey, everyone. I was hoping to have a look around." She's the same age as the grad students but seems much older right now. Lyla looks around. The sun hitting the canyon walls, turning the sandstone golden. "It looks different than Zion canyon."

"That's because this one runs east-west. There's more sunlight." Dana warms up. She loves talking about the canyons.

"And people lived in here?"

Dana nods. "They farmed here because the light was better. They only went into Zion to hunt and gather because it gets less sun for growing."

Lyla lifts her face to the sky. "I forgot how peaceful it is back here. Except for that construction, of course." She stands for a few moments, eyes closed. We watch her. It seems like she's meditating, but it's kind of odd to randomly do that in the middle of a conversation.

"What is she doing?" I whisper to Carter.

He shrugs. "Only Lyla knows the ways of Lyla."

We walk over to the archaeological site, where the interns all try to tell her about the pottery shards at once and who lived here, when. "This is a fascinating history," Lyla says. "I can't believe it's not some kind of national historic site."

"Us either." Dana smiles at her. "Are you interested in conservation?"

"I always loved going to the national parks when I was a kid. That was our summer thing—camping." Lyla lifts her face up to the sun again.

"I can't imagine you roughing it," Cass says. "Maybe glamping?"

Lyla shrugs. "I do sometimes. I mean, I consider this a work trip." She points to her face. "So I've got to get in my 'uniform.' But believe it or not, there are times when I go off the grid and don't even take a single photo of what I'm doing."

"That's so awesome," Carter says, as if Lyla Redding had invented cheese.

Grant and Dana and I walk her back to where the ferrets live. Their area's been cordoned off with tape. Reggie's squatting down by burrows, taking measurements. He's got a tent set up nearby.

"Reggie!" I call. "Hi!"

He stands up, pushing his black hair off his deep brown forehead. "Hey, it's Tuesday!"

We walk over and introduce Lyla. "How's it going?" Dana asks.

"Found a couple more burrows up here." He looks around. "It's unusual that the ferrets are here, but nothing is usual anymore. Things move around and live places where they wouldn't normally live because of people taking their habitat."

Dana explains the whole situation to Lyla from start to finish. I don't need to listen; I know the details already. But Lyla listens intently and asks questions. She nods a few times as if she's thinking about something, or wheels are turning in her head.

It's time for me to tell her my idea. "So I was thinking . . ."

"We were thinking," Carter prompts.

"We were thinking that if you could, you know, call on all your followers and tell them to sign a petition, or come here and protest, and post about it, then we could make them stop the development," I say.

We wait. I'm actually holding my breath. The adults

aren't saying anything, either, watching Lyla for a reaction.

"Hmmm." Lyla takes out her phone and begins snapping pictures. "Tuesday, will you send me all the photos you have of this place?"

I nod. Beside me Carter shifts, probably wishing that he got to send Lyla photos. I'm not sure what he thinks will happen with her. She's way too old for him.

"Great. I have an idea."

"With your followers?" I wrinkle my brow.

"No. It's going to take a few weeks, and I'm going to have to call some people, but I think I can do something bigger than that." She smiles as if she just heard some good news.

"Like what?" I ask.

She hesitates. "I don't want to get ahead of myself. I'm here because of you, Tuesday."

"Me?" I don't understand.

"You know how I said I'd put a bid in on the ranch? Well, all your photos of it and hearing about the ferrets make me want to try again." Lyla's got a glint in her eye, a determined expression that looks familiar. I try to place it.

Oh. She looks like Uncle Ezra did when he tried to do anything big.

My heart swells up several sizes. "But how?"

Lyla explains. She has a nonprofit foundation that

would actually do the purchase. "I would keep part of it for commercial use—build a restaurant with a small hotel, keep the rock-climbing area—and leave the valley as it is." She tosses her hair back. "It's just a matter of my lawyers talking to the developer's lawyers."

"But they're already continuing with the development. Why would they sell now?" Grant asks.

"Well. Maybe this is where my fan base comes into it." She whips out her phone and takes a video as we stand awkwardly in the background. "If you care about conservation, then you'll want to protest this. Petition link is in my profile." She repeats it in a different tone and angle, then ends the video. "There. I'll edit it and put it on TikTok and Instagram. Done." Lyla smiles brightly at us.

This is exactly what I've been hoping for. *More* than I was hoping for. A protest and her offering to buy?

"Let's see what happens now," Grant says.

I hold out my hand, and Lyla shakes it like we're in business together. "Thank you."

CHAPTER

39

A few weeks pass. Lyla posts a petition: *Sign to stop development at Hedges Ranch.* Her "Red-Pack Nation" swings into action. In a week, ten thousand people sign. In two weeks, twenty thousand. I really want something to happen before I have to move.

I keep looking for news coverage, but never see anything. Dana says that if it's a slow news day, they might do a story—otherwise the news devotes itself to major catastrophes and elections and things like that.

During the third week, Lyla starts dating some football player and the Red-Pack Nation starts talking about *that* instead. The petition stalls. Only a few people per day sign it now.

"What do you think it means?" I ask Dana. "Could they really forget about Hedges that fast?" We're sorting through our books, deciding what to donate and what to take with us to South Dakota. It's hard. So far, we've only chosen two to donate. Our move is starting to feel more real, as Dana shows me houses we could rent, and we try to figure out what part of town we want to live in. But I don't think I'll stop hoping we won't move, that something miraculous will happen and change Dana's mind.

"I don't know," Dana says. "Unless it was on the news or picked up momentum somehow, the internet always moves on to new things."

"They should care about this more than who Lyla's getting ice cream with." I haven't heard from Lyla. Somehow I thought she'd send me updates, but I don't really know why she would.

"They're just fans who like her photos. None of them want to do any work." Dana gives me a sympathetic smile.

I nod glumly. I don't know what else we could do to stop Hedges.

"Oh. I got an email from the Hedges owner about the ashes." Dana asked if we could scatter his ashes there.

"I assume it's not a yes," I say. "Because you would've told me right away."

"Correct. They say, '*If we let you do it, then everyone will want to do it,*'" she reads.

"Oof." My shoulders slump as disappointment hits me. Maybe I shouldn't be crushed, because either way Ezra is gone, but it feels like this is one last thing I could've done for my uncle. "Can we sneak over and do it anyway? I mean, how would they know?"

"They wouldn't. We could. But we won't." Dana smiles ruefully. "We'll do something else with them. Something he would've liked. Things don't always work out the way we want."

"You mean they never work out the way I want," I say darkly.

"I know what you mean," my mother says, and for some reason that helps. "What about this book?" Dana holds one up. It's a book from the eighties about *dressing in your color season* or something. *"Dress for success by determining your seasonal palette,"* she reads.

We look at each other and roll our eyes at exactly the same time. "Donate," we both say at once, and then laugh.

There's one good thing that's happened since we decided to do something with Ezra's ashes. I think my mother's finally coming back to me.

The next morning, I go over to Carter's. The moving truck sits in the driveway, and Grant and Carter's mom and some other people are loading it up. Tomorrow, very early, they'll drive the truck out of here and head for North Carolina.

For now, Carter is taking a break, and we've set up the tripod and camera for a few last photos. Carter wanted to take a picture of this vista, this view, one last time—Watchman across the valley.

Now we're lying on our backs in his front yard, the adults noisily laughing and clattering around inside and out. If I reach out my arm and he reaches out his, we can barely touch our fingertips. "What do you think is going on with the Hedges deal?" I say.

"I have no idea. Red-Pack Nation didn't make a difference." Carter sits up on his elbow.

"I feel like she was a big maybe anyway. And Uncle Ezra always said maybe is usually a no." I pull up a piece of grass, watching Jenny carry a box to the truck. It feels wrong for both me and Carter to leave Zion before we know the answer to this question.

"Well, let's google the news." Carter's on his phone.

"I've done that," I say.

"Did you do it today?"

"No," I admit. "Want me to come help?" I call to Jenny.

She shakes her head and goes to the house. "We've got it. You two keep playing."

We're way too old to play. But I guess moms have to mom.

"Look at this." Carter shows me. It's an article by that lady who interviewed me. *"Development Continuing Despite Endangered Animals and Petition,"* I read out loud. "Presales of homes beginning?" I add the question mark.

"That doesn't sound like Lyla's deal went through," Carter points out.

"That must be why she didn't answer me. She couldn't make it happen." Anger rears up. Why did she even mention it unless she was sure? That's like promising a kid a trip to Disneyland and then backing out. I take out my phone and message Lyla again.

I read the article that says home pre-sales are starting, I type. *Does this mean the deal didn't go through?? Or do they not know you're buying it?*

I send it and show it to Carter. "Whoa, two question marks? You sound mad."

"I'm not mad. Well, maybe a little. Really? That's what two mean?" I'm not totally familiar with all the ways of texting.

Carter nods. "Yeah."

I add, *It's okay to tell me no.* Maybe she's worried about me being heartbroken. I mean, well, she's not wrong if she thinks that.

"There must be another way to contact her," Carter says. "She probably doesn't see all her Instagram messages."

"What else is there?" I ask.

"A manager or something."

We both google her. *Lyla Redding contact information.* One hit comes up: a talent agency in Los Angeles.

Represented by Miles Galliant. "What if I email her agent?"

"Why would he respond to you, like ever? It's easy to ignore an email." Carter sets his jaw. "No. Grant says the best way to get an answer is to call them."

My heart tries to squeeze out of my throat. I don't like making phone calls. On phones, I've got no faces to look at, no hand gestures. I always misinterpret emotions on the phone. "Will you do it?"

"I could. What do you want me to say?" Carter holds his hand out. He's not afraid of anything.

"Ask about the deal."

Carter looks at the phone number on my screen, dials it on his phone. It rings. "Um, yeah, hi, can I talk to, uh . . ."

"Miles," I say.

"Miles. Or is it kilometers?" Carter giggles nervously. Uh-oh. Random dad jokes? This is not going well. Carter turns red as he realizes what he blurted out. "Um, yeah. Who's calling? Um . . . This is Carter . . . No, no. I don't know him . . . Oh yeah. No, I understand. Okay. Bye." He hangs up.

I realize I'm clenching my nails into my palms. "What did they say?"

"He's busy."

"They didn't even take a message," I point out.

"Yeah." Carter's still red. "I kind of messed that up. I'm sorry."

"That's okay," I say, because after all I was too scared to even try. Ezra said the best way to deal with a situation where you don't feel sure of yourself is to pretend that you're sure.

I can do this. I swallow. "I'll call. I've done harder things." When I say this aloud, I know it's true. Climbing that rock looking for owls was harder than this. This is nothing.

"We could ask Dana or my parents to call," Carter says.

"No." I want to do it now. I dial before I can change my mind. "Galliant Talent," a woman says pleasantly into the phone. "How may I help you?"

I make my voice as serious as possible. I pretend that I'm an adult white man like Uncle Ezra, who doesn't care what this lady or anybody else thinks of him. I am Tuesday Beals, and I own the world, I think grandly to myself. "Tuesday Beals for Miles Galliant, please."

"One moment." She puts me on hold.

I widen my eyes at Carter.

"Miles Galliant here," a deep voice says at the other end. "Ms. Beals, how are you?"

"I'm fine," I answer, still holding on to the ultra-confidence. "I'm calling you because I am involved with your client Lyla Redding and the purchase of Hedges Ranch."

"Lyla Redding? Wait, where are you from?" he asks.

"I'm in Zion National Park," I say.

"I thought you were with a production company." He sounds confused. "Oh, you want her nonprofit foundation. Let me give you that number." He dictates it to me, and I hold the phone away from my ear so Carter can hear it and punch the numbers into his.

"Thanks," I say. "Have a great day." I hang up.

"Wow," Carter says. "You sounded like a legit adult."

I grin. "I know." I take his phone and hit the green button.

I try the same thing with the charity, but it's harder here because I don't know who I need to talk to even. The receptionist actually asks, "May I ask why you're calling?"

I take a breath. "I'm Tuesday Beals. I'm the kid Lyla talked to here at Zion. I just want to know what's going on with the deal to buy Hedges."

"Oh, Tuesday. The girl from the ranch. This is Liz, Lyla's assistant. How are you?"

"Hi, I'm fine, thank you," I say, remembering that Lyla said they were pretty much the same person.

"You're on my list of people to contact, actually." Liz clears her throat. She sounds nervous. "It's, uh, over."

"What do you mean?"

"They didn't accept the offer. It's over," she repeats.

My stomach flips. "That's it?"

Carter scoots closer to me, his eyebrows up, waiting.

"That's it," she says through a sad little sigh. "I'm sorry it didn't work out."

I pluck a blade of grass out of the dirt. "Yeah. Me too."

"How about I send you a package of Lyla's products?" Liz offers. "The whole line."

"No thank you," I say with a shudder. I just want to get off the phone now. "That's the last thing in the world I want."

"Oh. Okay." She has a nervous little chuckle. "Maybe a membership to the Audubon? Lyla wants to do something nice for you."

"She doesn't need to do anything for me," I say, and I mean it. This is the only thing I will ever want from Lyla Redding in my whole life. "I have to go." Liz says goodbye, and I finally hang up. I turn to Carter and I don't even have to say anything—he already knew from my face. He wraps his arms around me for a fierce hug, and I let him.

CHAPTER

40

"I kind of wish Lyla hadn't said anything at all," I say to Carter. "It's so disappointing."

"I know." Carter sighs. "I know."

Having him agree with me makes me feel a tiny bit better. I guess you can't win them all. That sounds like something Uncle Ezra might say, except he never did—because Ezra generally thought he could win everything, all the time. Except you can't.

That is a fact, and I always have to accept facts even if I don't like them.

But right now, Carter is still here with me, and I have to enjoy the last minutes we're having together. "Let's get our minds off that. What's your favorite fruit?" he asks.

"You know what my favorite fruit is. Blackberries in the summer. That's a random question."

Carter types this in a note on his phone. "What about in the fall?"

"Apple. And then tangelo in the winter. They're in season in Florida in December." I turn to look at him. The light hits his lashes, making them sort of glow. "Why do you r. ed to know all this?"

"I don't want to forget." He flashes me a quick smile. "I want to remember everything about you."

"We can video chat. It's not like the olden days when people only had technology like this." I gesture at the camera.

"It's not the same," Carter says. He sniffs. "They don't have Smell-O-Vision video chat. I can't smell which type of sunblock you have on or that you had garlic bread for lunch."

"You know I always use the same sunblock, except if I use yours." I laugh, because today we both had garlic breath for lunch, and his garlic breath is strong, too, though we're lying two arms' lengths away from each other. "But yeah. It's not the same."

We look up at the sky, the blue so intense it makes me squint. A yellow-bellied warbler sings his song. Two hawks circle the sky, their tan feathers polka-dotted with brown. "I think those are Cooper's hawks."

"I think you're right." He sits all the way up and wipes at his face. "I'm going to miss you, Tuesday. You've been my best friend for four years."

"I'm going to miss you, too." It still hurts that he'll be gone, but I'll be gone, too, soon enough.

He lies back down. We stay like this for a while, watching the hawks until one suddenly swoops down, the other one following, until Grant comes out and tells Carter it's time to get back to work.

We both stand. "So. This is it," Carter says.

I nod. At first I think I'm all cried out from earlier, but this hits me, too. If I say anything, I'll start bawling again. But Carter looks at me expectantly, and I can't say nothing at all. "Don't forget about me."

"Never."

I think about hugging him again but I really can't, or I'll lose it. Instead, I hold out my hand and Carter shakes it. Then I turn and walk away, not looking back, and when I get to the underpass, I start running home so I can cry in private.

CHAPTER
41

T he first week Carter is gone, I wake up every morning wondering what I should do, and not wanting to do anything except sit around feeling sorry for myself. Everything I've done this summer has been kind of useless. Yes, I found the ferrets, but Lyla couldn't buy the ranch, and it's still getting developed.

Uncle Ezra's urn stares at me from the mantel. Dana says she can get a special permit to spread his ashes out in Zion instead. "It's not ideal, but it's better than nothing," she told me. She promised we'll do it soon, before we leave.

After breakfast during that first week, I go to where I can get a cell signal and check to see if Carter texted and what's going on in my Instagram. Carter usually does text with a photo of where they are on their trip across the country, so that's always nice. But on Instagram, the activity is going down, and I don't have any new photos to post. I stop getting likes, and this makes me even more depressed, though it didn't affect anything anyway.

Then, after seven days of feeling low, I realize that I already know what I want to do. More photography. I want to take photographs without worrying about posting them anywhere.

"Dana," I say to my mother on the eighth morning after Carter left, while she and I are sorting through the stuff in the hall closet for our move, "I think social media is messing with my head."

"Delete it," she says promptly. "It did all the good it's going to do."

I delete my Instagram app but leave the account up, so people can still see the photos but I don't have to worry about numbers. I start visiting Danielle more, like every day more, and she shows me techniques for making different areas of the photos have more detail.

And one night, she takes me out to shoot the sky, and I set up my telescope for her so she can see the planets in detail. I show her how to use my astronomy camera, and she shows me how to use a regular camera to capture what we see from Earth. "Just fabulous!" Danielle says after I show her Jupiter. She teaches me how to use Photoshop to make art, like CheddarBunny—to add colors and filters in order to make the planets pop. It's actually amazing, this art—and soon I'm adding my versions to the art pages on ClearNights.

Every time I go to Danielle's art studio, I pass Hedges. Every time, there's more work being done on the building in front—it's going to block the whole natural entrance to the ranch. You can't even tell there's land behind it anymore.

Myra and Reggie haven't found any more black-footed ferrets, though it'll take them months to survey the whole ranch, but sometimes a few protestors show up with signs saying *Keep Zion Dark!* And I wonder if I should join them. But Dana says that's not something I should go to by myself.

Then, one afternoon in early August, maybe a week and a half after I talked to Lyla's assistant, Danielle and I are having coffee on the patio at the shop across from her studio. We're checking out planetary photos on her laptop, and she's showing me how to use Photoshop. "Perfect," I say, and draw a line around a prairie dog photo, cutting it from one image, and then pasting the animal to an image of the moon. I'm sending this to Myra. I chuckle to myself.

A familiar-looking news van rolls up in the dirt parking lot, kicking up tan sand. Danielle and I stop working. "What's going on?" I wonder out loud.

Shelby the news reporter gets out and crosses to the patio where the entrance is, looking fresh and polished as if she didn't just have a four-hour drive from Salt Lake City. "Well, if it isn't Tuesday Beals, girl wonder." She smiles at me.

I squint back at her. "What are you doing in town again?"

"Covering the biggest story in the state." Shelby grins. "Haven't you heard?"

I shake my head. "I haven't been on the internet in a while."

"Oh, really?" Shelby sits down in the chair next to me and pulls out her phone. "Let me be the first to share." She shows me a news article.

LYLA REDDING BUYS HEDGES RANCH

In a stunning development, 24-year-old cosmetics mogul Lyla Redding has swooped in and purchased Hedges Ranch from the developers, who had already begun work. Details are being kept under wraps until the purchase is finalized. A spokesperson for Redding said, "Lyla has a long history of conservation and looks forward to being a caretaker of this important natural resource."

"Um, what?" I can't believe this is true. I must be dreaming. "They said yes? But how? Why? How much?"

"Well, it'll be in the public record soon enough."

Shelby takes her phone back. "First, Lyla offered them a fair amount—five million more than they paid. Thirty million. They turned it down."

I gulp. "That's so much money."

"To you and me, thirty million's a huge amount," Danielle says. "A billionaire has so much money that thirty million's like buying a coffee."

I can't imagine why anyone would ever need to have that much money. "But the nonprofit said the deal didn't go through!"

Shelby leans forward. "Yes. That's what happened a few weeks ago. However, something made Lyla go back to them with a new offer last week. Thirty-five million. Plus, a new wrinkle." Shelby smiles at us smugly. Obviously she's the only one who knows the whole story. "So the appeal that the developer had with the state to continue construction got overturned. The state ruled—with finality—that they have to stop *all* construction and survey the entire land for wildlife, and that could take months and months. With a delay that long, they stood to lose money, so they took it."

I stare at her in openmouthed wonder.

"Don't worry about Lyla spending too much money. Lyla's nonprofit foundation is buying it, so it's good for her financially, too. Win-win." She smiles. "It wouldn't have happened without you, Tuesday."

I frown at her, remembering the questions she asked last time. "I thought you wanted the development to happen."

"I'm a reporter. I have to ask the contrary questions." Shelby shrugs. "Anyway, I've got to get going. I wanted to say congratulations." She stands.

"Thanks." I still feel like this isn't happening.

Shelby disappears into the coffee shop, and Danielle turns to me. "Isn't that amazing? You do deserve the credit."

"I didn't do that much," I say. "I started out by looking for archaeological sites."

"But that was enough to get you started on the right trail, even though you didn't know it at the time and everything went differently than you thought." Danielle smiles. "Gosh, isn't life full of surprises?"

I guess Danielle is right. It's like what those scientists Ezra talked about did—started with a different goal and ended up somewhere else maybe even better. At the start of summer, my goal was to find a new comet, not look for archaeological sites or save a ranch.

Maybe it shows you have to be open to changing what you're looking for, when you get new information. If I'd kept up with my only goal, I never would have met Danielle or Silas or anything, and I never would have found the ferrets. "Yep. Life is," I say to her.

I download Instagram again and send Lyla a message.

Congrats on the deal. Thank you for trying again. Then I text Carter. *Guess what??* Oh—now I get the whole two question mark thing.

Awesome!! Carter responds immediately.

Danielle reaches out her hand, and I take it. "I'm so glad I got the chance to know you, Tuesday. You're a special person."

That makes me feel all warm inside. Uncle Ezra, the one person besides my mother who always told me I was special, is gone. But Danielle still exists, and maybe there will be new people to meet in South Dakota like her and Carter and Silas. I can only hope. "Same," I say to Danielle.

Later, I'm in Dana's office, bouncing up and down on the ball as I read a book (Dana doesn't understand how I don't get motion sick) when I get a notification of a new message on Instagram. It's Lyla.

Honestly, I'd given up completely. But my agent and the nonprofit both told me you called. It made me feel like I'd let you down. Not to mention the whole bigger picture. So I decided to give it one more try. Somehow the stars aligned the second time.

I double-tap her message, hearting it. I hadn't thought I was doing anything special when I called her offices. I was trying to find out information. But somehow, my little action had an impact. I look at her message, and

I'm reminded of an astronomical event that's going to take place. *Did you know that this December, Jupiter and Saturn and their moons will actually align and it will be the only time you can see them in your entire life with just your eyeballs?*

She double-taps the message. *Then I guess I'll view it from Hedges. Thanks, Tuesday.*

42

A t sunset in mid-August, we drive into Hedges, just me and Dana. It's quiet now, with the construction stopped and the press gone. Lyla's building a restaurant at the entrance, with a small farm in the back that will provide the vegetables. She'll have rock climbing, and people can apply for camping and hiking permits. But other than that—

Nothing.

A whole lot of nothing. Which is how it should be.

Lyla's told me I can come back whenever I like. *I'm going to build a little artist's cabin, too,* she tells me in an Instagram message. *I'll stay in it when I'm here, and you can use it, too, when you visit. For free.*

Lyla is nicer than I thought she'd be.

Our house is all packed up and ready to go. Tomorrow Dana and I will drive out to South Dakota, and our stuff will follow. She's already rented a little house for us—complete with internet.

Carter's been settled for weeks now and has sent me photos of his house and the Great Smoky Mountains National Park in North Carolina. It's got more green than Utah does—it rains a whole lot more. *Can't wait to show you this place*, Carter wrote. He texts or emails almost every day.

Dana and I drive until the road inside Hedges ends, then pull over. We strap on our CamelBaks. I make sure my hiking shoes are securely tied, which is also a thing Ezra did for me. Then we climb.

It's August 12, the day of the Perseid meteor shower.

I snap a selfie for Carter, making a face. Dana pops into the picture, giving me rabbit ears. "Dana!" I say with a laugh. But I like the photo. We look happy, my mother and me. I send it to him before we lose signal.

Lol, Carter responds immediately. *Have fun.*

We will, I type back.

We go up the trail. I remember Uncle Ezra taking me to the head. It begins right above the bend in the river. If we had taken the left fork, we would go to where the ferrets are. Instead we take the fork to the right. With every step I take, I flash back to walking behind Ezra. The sounds of us breathing hard, his big heavy boots plodding in the dirt. Then I blink and I'm behind Dana instead.

And then the boulders. I look up at them.

A worn path goes up through these rocks. There are two, one stacked on the other like a stair, and then a small opening into who-knows-what beyond. I can't see past that.

I remember it being steep and scary-looking when Ezra took me here, as if I'd fall to my doom as soon as I climbed up. Now it doesn't look so bad. That there are natural hand- and footholds for us to use.

Last year, I couldn't see the path. This year I do, as if it's been marked out for me.

Carter says seeing the way up is called "problem solving" in bouldering. I guess that's what I did. "Come on," I say to Dana and lead the way.

"I'll catch you if you slip," she says.

"I'm almost as big as you. I'll knock you over."

"It doesn't matter. I'm your mother. I won't let you fall."

For whatever reason, I couldn't make myself follow Ezra up over these boulders. It wasn't that I didn't trust him. I did. I thought we both might fall, with nobody to help us. Or that I'd get stuck and scared. "It's okay," he said. "There's always next year. We'll do it when you're ready."

The sun's going down. It's starting to set earlier these days as we head into fall. I turn on my red headlamp, Dana doing the same, and squeeze through the opening. Beyond, there are more boulders to climb. Great. An owl flies out from the cliffs somewhere, calling its four bark-ing hoots, huge against the violet-pink sky. *Beyond the owl's pinions.*

We continue up. Sandstone is always covered in grit as sand continually comes off the stone. Sand is slippery, and sometimes my boots slide out from under me. Dana's hand steadies me every single time. "Got it?" she says.

"Yup." I peer over my shoulder back to her and wish I hadn't. We're a long way up. There are no chains to hold on to like there are at Angels Landing, no park rangers ready to radio in help. There's only me and Dana.

That's enough. We are enough.

"Almost there," Dana says.

I see the top ahead and climb up eagerly.

This is a mesa. Table. *The table where we ate.* I think about the other mesa where we'd camped. He'd known I would think of the other place first—a misleading clue, aka a red herring, as it's called in mysteries. He'd wanted me to think of that place first, but I needed Dana to fin-ish Ezra's riddle.

I bet he wanted it that way. Maybe he knew how his sister would react to his passing, how closed off she'd be and how lonely I'd feel, and pushed us to work together in the most Ezra way possible. I smile at the thought.

But he probably hadn't known I would think it was an archaeological site. Sometimes things work out the way you least expect.

Like Danielle said, life is full of surprises.

I scramble over the last angled rock, then turn and offer a hand to my mother.

She takes it. I brace myself on the boulder and haul her up. I've gotten stronger this summer, I realize. A lot stronger. I shake the dust off my hands and look around.

The mesa is big. Not as big as the top of Watchmen, but as big as a living room. A few small pines dot the landscape. It's like a private campground.

The air's cooler up here. The stars are beginning to glimmer in the sky. It feels like I could reach up and touch them, as if we're in a cozy planetarium instead of out in the open. Protected and sheltered.

The same feeling I got when I was with Ezra. I shiver. *Where the sky lives.*

Dana feels it, too, because she sits down quietly beside me and we're quiet together. Both thinking of Ezra. Remembering him. Dana feels warm next to me, and I think of how she's my only blood family now. So Carter's my family, too, and so are Jenny and Grant, and even Danielle and Silas. Like Danielle's husband said, these are all people whom I'd trust to watch my theoretical puppy and whom I like.

"I miss him so much." My voice sounds loud in the dark and still of the wilderness.

Dana leans into me. "I do, too."

We sit for a while longer, looking at the stars. I name

them in my head, the constellations, the planets, exactly as if Ezra is here.

Then, suddenly, the meteor shower begins as Earth passes through the field of comet and asteroid debris, and these rocks burn brightly as they hit our atmosphere. This shower comes from the Perseus constellation, so it's called Perseid. All the meteors come from a central point inside Perseus—the radius—and shoot in all directions. They ping out, over and over again, and it's better than any fireworks show I've seen. Plus, it's quiet.

"Ready?" Dana asks at last, and I nod. It's time.

She takes the bag of Ezra's ashes out of the backpack, and we go to the edge of the mesa. Below is nothing but darkness, because Hedges has no buildings. Above are the stars.

The two of us are so tiny compared to the sky, to the universe. If the universe were a body we'd be smaller than ants on it. Nothing more than the smallest specks. But here together, we're okay. We have a place.

We stand with our backs to the wind. Dana hands me the bag and I open it, and then she puts her hand over mine, and together, as if we're one person, we release him back to the sky. To the meteors and the comets and the stars.

The stars are where we come from. And now Carter's mom is making a new human child out of them and Ezra's going back.

Ezra is dead, and that is a fact. But so are many of these stars. They're so far away, trillions and trillions of miles, that what's visible from Earth is already in the past. The stars died off a long time ago. The same dead stars Ezra and I looked at. It shouldn't make me feel better to know they're dead, but it does.

Because even when they're gone, someone still sees their light.

ACKNOWLEDGMENTS

It always takes more than one person to write a novel, and in this case, it took a national park. When I had the opportunity to live in Zion National Park in Utah for a whole month as the Artist-in-Residence, I got to know the inner workings of the park and got to pick the brains of a few folks, including: Courtney Mackay, the Cultural Resource Manager; Janice Stroud-Settles, the Wildlife Program Manager; Samuel Davis, Assistant Professor of Photography at Southern Utah University; and Eleanor Siebers, the Volunteer Program Manager. Any mistakes I made were my own. Thanks also to Miriam Watson, Museum Curator, who was also on the committee that chose me. Thanks also to archaeologist Dr. Alia Wallace who helped launch me down this path.

Conservation shouldn't be political, but it often is. Currently, the state's governor and senators oppose the use of a ticketing system to limit the number of people coming into Zion, preferring to use the park as a state revenue source while not giving them the appropriate means to manage the crowds. Go to the National Parks Foundation (www.nationalparks.org) to find out how to support your favorite parks.